KING ARTHUR
AND
THE ROUND TABLE

For Sir Riley
G. M.

Text copyright © Geraldine McCaughrean 1996
Illustrations copyright © Alan Marks 1996

First published in Great Britain in 1996 by
Macdonald Young Books
This edition published 2006
by Hodder Children's Books
a division of Hodder Headline Limited
338 Euston Road, London NW1 3BH

British Library Cataloguing in Publication Data available.
ISBN 0 340 89437 7

10 9 8 7 6 5 4 3 2 1

Printed and bound in Great Britain by Bookmarque Ltd

KING ARTHUR
AND
THE ROUND TABLE

A LEGEND RETOLD BY

GERALDINE MCCAUGHREAN

ILLUSTRATED BY ALAN MARKS

Hodder
Children's
Books

A division of Hodder Headline Limited

One

THE
PRICE OF SIN

$\mathcal{D}$ragonheaded Uther they called him, because there was fire in his blood and a spark in his eye. Dragons had flown through the skies declaring his right to the crown of Albion. His temper was hot, but his love was unswerving, as his best friends could vouch. And his best friend of all was the magician Merlin.

When passionate King Uther chanced to see a woman more beautiful than he had ever seen before, he fixed all his hopes on her. No matter that she was married, and to Gorlais, a venerable nobleman in Uther's own court. No matter that her husband shut her up for safe keeping in a towering black castle moated by the sea. Uther longed for the fair Igrayne as a starving man longs for food.

So he picked a groundless quarrel with old Sir Gorlais,

and made war on him. The two armies camped, face-to-face, in preparation for battle, while Igrayne trembled in her salt-moated castle.

'Help me, Merlin! Help me to win her!' said Uther. In the distance, the black turrets of Tintagel spiralled into the twilit sky above a sheet-metal sea.

'It would be a sin,' said Merlin, 'and sins always have a price.'

'I'll pay it! Whatever the price, I'll pay it! Only let me hold that woman in my arms!' And Merlin (who could see the future like the view from a window) knew that the sin must be allowed to happen.

So he used magic to disguise Uther as Igrayne's husband. The King's eyes wrinkled and sank into their sockets. His features melted and drooped into those of old Sir Gorlais.

'A child will be born because of this night,' said Merlin. 'It will be born to the Lady Igrayne, and you will be the father. I want that boy, to raise up and rear. He has a job to do, and I will train him for it. That is my fee,' said Merlin.

'You're welcome to him if I can just have her,' Uther replied, unthinking in his impatience.

So while the real Sir Gorlais slept, unsuspecting, beside a soldier's camp fire, his *likeness* rode at midnight across the causeway and in at Tintagel's gate.

'Halt, who goes there?' The guard peered into Uther's

face. 'Oh! Good evening, master. Have you fought the King already? Is he driven off?'

'Not yet, not yet,' muttered the figure on horseback. 'I had a mind to visit my wife before tomorrow's battle. So here I am. As you see.' The guard let him pass, believing he was seeing the castle's owner ride in under its portcullis.

Uther could not declare his love to the lovely Igrayne. In fact he hardly dared speak a word to her, for fear his voice betrayed who he really was. Igrayne was a virtuous woman, and would never have opened her door to a man other than her lawful husband. But that night, of course, she thought she was kissing her husband when she kissed his likeness, and she thought she was touching Sir Gorlais when the man lay down beside her. She sensed some change, some difference . . . Gorlais had never been so tender or so passionate. But she could never have imagined it was Dragonheaded Uther she held in her arms: Merlin's magic was far too perfect.

Uther stayed much longer than he meant to. He left much later than he should. Outside, the warm morning sun melted Merlin's magic, and it was Dragonheaded Uther's face which turned to the sky and sang with happiness. He had held his beloved Igrayne in his arms; he had achieved his heart's desire.

Back at Tintagel, a messenger came to Igrayne's

chamber. 'Oh lady, lady, lady! The worst news! The worst! Your husband is dead.'

'How? When? Where?' gasped Igrayne. 'He has only just . . .'

'Three hours since, on the battlefield,' replied the messenger, 'killed in a skirmish with Uther's men.'

The Lady Igrayne fell to the ground with a cry. It was hardly to be wondered at, only to be expected. But Igrayne never revealed the true reason for her faint. It could not have been Gorlais who spent the night in her bed. And that was one secret she must keep to herself for ever.

Over by the narrow slitted window, hearing the messenger's words, Gorlais' little daughter – Morgan – opened her mouth and screamed. It was such a scream as crazed the ice in the yard and blasted the Christmas roses. She shed no tears and she sighed no sigh. But she swore to hate Dragonheaded Uther for ever and to be revenged on him. '*Let him have a son*,' little Morgan wished on the morning star. '*Let him have a son*,' she begged of the faeries, '*so that I can be revenged on him for the death of my father!*'

Sir Gorlais was dead. Uther seized on Igrayne, like a prize won at tournament, marrying her before the year was out, before she even gave birth to their son.

When that child was one year old, Merlin held Uther to his promise, and took the tiny boy from his parents –

rode with him deep into forests, far away from court, far away from the mischief which had begun him. They rode through the vales of Faeryland and the magic lakelands and gorges, through the lairs of dragons and the battlefields of the Dead.

At last, he entrusted the child into the keeping of Sir Ector, a poor knight with a good heart and a kind wife. The couple already had one son; another would pass for his brother. They would have done as much for any orphan brought to the door on a cold night: they had no idea where the boy came from.

Merlin told no one, not even Uther or Igrayne, what had become of the child. All they knew was that once they had had a son and called him Arthur, and that now he was gone. It was a small thing to lose from their lives – larger than a puppy but smaller than a saddle. Yet they grieved for him with a terrible grief.

Morgan no longer had the baby at hand to hate, so she turned her hatred back on Uther. She mixed a potion of henbane and foxglove, mistletoe and snowberries. And she served it to her stepfather, as he pored over maps and battle strategies, beneath the candles of Tintagel's hall.

Morgan heard her stepfather sigh. Every day Saxon invaders advanced farther into his territories, and he scowled with worry as he charted their progress across the maps. Deep in thought, he drank deeply from Morgan's cup.

Then he died, face-down among his maps, face-down among his enemies. And Morgan smiled, wiped the poisoned cup with her long hair, and silently left the room.

Two

THE SWORD
IN THE ANVIL

The Saxons rejoiced in the fall of Dragonheaded Uther. They swept ashore, fleet after fleet, insolent and greedy for plunder. Who was left to repulse them, after all? A rabble of warlords, more intent on fighting each other than fighting off Saxons; all vying for the crown and none of them man enough to wear it.

Merlin watched the warlords squabble and the Saxons chew and mangle England, but he shed no tears. He drew breath slowly, as the hills breathe, and his heart beat with the slow, inexorable thud of a blacksmith's hammer falling on the anvil amid a cloud of sparks.

'Hurry, boy, hurry! What's keeping you?' Sir Ector was agitated. His elder son was to fight in the Christmas jousts for the first time – in London! He might be hurt or he might be noticed. He might come home covered in bruises or covered in glory. And so Sir Ector scolded and clucked at his younger son – 'Hurry up! Is everything ready?' – getting in the way and making the boy's work harder.

Arthur was squire to his elder brother, Kay, and it was for him to make certain Sir Kay was perfectly accoutred for the tournament, his armour polished, the hinges oiled, the horse groomed, his bundle of lances lashed together. He had given Kay some sword practice and served him breakfast and held the mirror for him while he combed his beard. Arthur was too young to have a beard, and he envied Kay's. He envied him his chance to fight at Westminster, too, but knew that envy was a vice, and put it out of his mind. All in good time, his own chance would come.

They had a long journey up to London and arrived late. Their overnight lodging was expensive and flea-ridden, but late-comers had to take what they could find. The city was crowded with visitors.

But round the corner, beyond the Abbey-church, the tourney field was bright with pennons, pavilions and the stripe-painted facias of the grandstands. Women dressed as colourfully as a field of flowers shrieked excitedly and leaned their heads together to giggle. Knights picked quarrels with one another, to put themselves in fighting mood. Kay reorganized his pleasant features into a fierce

grimace. 'Now give me my sword, Arthur, and watch what I can do!'

'Your sword, yes. Isn't it in your saddle-sheath?'

Arthur ran to the horse. The sheath hung empty. He ran to the pile of maces and clubs. No sword.

'Well, Arthur?' said his father. 'Where's Kay's sword? He can't compete without a sword, boy.'

'No, of course. I'm sure I . . . Yes, I'll just . . .' Arthur picked up his heels and ran – all the way back to the lodging-house. To have forgotten Kay's sword! It was a catastrophe his brother would never forgive him for.

He beat on the door, but nobody came. The landlady had gone out! He saw an open upper window, and climbed on to a cart, but he was not tall enough to reach the sill. He thought of buying a sword: he had no money. He thought of borrowing one, but on tournament day? Who would part with their weapon? He thought of stealing one, but that would have shamed both him and Kay.

On the precinct of Westminster Abbey-church, he prayed a fervent prayer: 'Oh God! Please give me a sword!'

And there it was. A big slab of rock, such as builders might abandon, lay in the long grass. On top of it was a blacksmith's anvil. And wedged into the anvil – a sword!

Somewhere a trumpet fanfare blew. Another few moments and Kay would be disqualified, disgraced, for

want of a sword. Arthur leapt on to the stone, braced his knees against the anvil and gripped the swordhilt. 'I'll fetch it back, I promise!' he said, aloud, thinking this might be a gravestone of some dead knight. The sword slipped out easily.

A woman passer-by stopped and stared, open-mouthed. 'A loan, that's all,' called Arthur apologetically, and ran. The passer-by stopped a man. Behind him Arthur could hear their shocked voices:

'Did you see?'

'That boy just . . .'

Arthur tore back along the street, the sword tucked under his arm for fear of running into someone. He was just in time. Another fanfare sounded, as he thrust the sword into his brother's hands.

Kay staggered. 'This isn't mine.'

'No. The lodgings . . . I'm sorry . . . found it.' Arthur was too out of breath to explain.

Kay slid the sword home into his saddle-sheath. The

sheath's stitching was instantly sliced through, and the bare sword fell to the ground. Kay picked it up. Arthur bit his lip.

The woman who had seen Arthur take the sword came pushing through the crowds. The man was close behind. 'That boy,' she said, pointing. 'He just took . . .'

'Oh pig's-feathers,' muttered Arthur and tried to melt out of sight.

But the crowd grew more and more noisy, more and more excitable. 'The boy pulled the sword out of the anvil! I tell you he did!'

'Don't be ridiculous!'

'I know what I saw!'

'Don't believe you.'

'Well, the sword's gone now, and there's the truth. That's it there!'

The stewards and heralds on the field of tourney noticed the disturbance and came asking questions. They found Kay surrounded by peasants and merchants and housewives, sullying his armour with their dirty fingers and saying, 'The boy pulled the sword out of the anvil!'

'This knight?'

Kay's eyes met his father's. He said nothing.

'No! T'other one. The boy. There!'

There was no escaping the huge circle of people which pressed in on Kay, Sir Ector, Arthur and the borrowed sword.

Sir Ector laid both hands on Arthur's shoulders. 'Tell me, Arthur. Where did you find the sword?'

'I'm sorry. I pulled it out of some anvil in a stone beside the Abbey. I meant to take it back after Kay . . . I never knew it would cause such a . . .' The crowd gave such a gasp that he faltered. The knights off the tourney field seemed unreasonably angry.

'Absurd.'

'It's a lie.'

'A fraud.'

The jostling crowds began moving back through the streets, the tournament forgotten. Kay and Arthur and Sir Ector were swept along by it. Kay still had hold of the borrowed sword.

'What have I done, father?' Arthur pleaded to know.

'Did you read the words carved on the stone, boy?' said Sir Ector. He seemed oddly calm.

'Words? No. The grass was long . . .'

In the Abbey precinct, the press of people round about the stone and anvil soon trod flat the long grass. Words carved around the base were uncovered one by one:

WHO PULLS . . . THIS ANVIL . . . OF ENGL . . .

A knight snatched the sword out of Kay's hand and staggered a little – 'a boy couldn't lift this' – as he pushed the blade back into the slot in the anvil. 'Now show us,' he sneered.

Arthur did not move. So Kay took hold of the

swordhilt and pulled till his face turned red. The sword did not budge.

An older, much grander knight shouldered him out of the way and hauled on the sword till his face turned purple and he griped at his stomach. But the sword did not budge. Arthur felt Sir Ector's hand on his shoulder, pushing him forward. He stepped up on to the rock and pulled out the sword as easily as a knife out of butter.

A silence like snowfall muffled everything. The crowd gaped up at him – a sea of round white faces all looking up. A single whispered word skipped like a stone across the surface of that sea:

'. . . *king . . . king . . . king . . .*'

Then the knights were blaring at him:

'Never!'

'Get down!'

'A farmboy with mud on his boots?'

Sir Ector read out the words in his mellow countryman's drawl: '*WHO PULLS THE SWORD FROM OUT THIS ANVIL IS THE TRUE AND RIGHTFUL KING OF ENGLAND.*'

For weeks the talk in London had been of nothing but the sword-in-the-anvil. It had appeared one morning from nowhere, without explanation or footprint nearby – as if dropped from the sky. The words round its base had aroused such ambitions in the hearts of local knights that they had queued in a line reaching right around the

Abbey, for their chance to pull on the swordhilt. Knights arriving early for the tournament heard rumours of the sword-in-the-anvil. But one by one they too had failed, and one by one they had blustered and snorted and declared the task impossible. The queue of knights dwindled to one, then to none.

Of course the rumours had not reached as far as Sir Ector's lands. Even so, Sir Ector and Kay had heard mention of the sword-in-the-anvil, among the gossips at the inn. Only Arthur had gone to bed at once, so as to be up and busy before dawn.

Now Sir Ector read the words off the base of the stone: '*WHO PULLS THE SWORD FROM OUT THIS ANVIL IS THE TRUE AND RIGHTFUL KING OF ENGLAND.*'

'And that's your little boy, is it?' jeered a knight who had served alongside Dragonheaded Uther. His chain-mail hissed liked a snake.

'I am not his father,' said Sir Ector. The tremor in his voice enthralled the crowd. 'Would that I were, for God knows I love the boy like a son.'

Up on his rock, Arthur felt marooned, a prisoner of events. Sir Ector not his father? This was the first he had heard of it. 'The magician Merlin brought him to me as a baby – an orphan he said, in need of a home. I see now what he brought me.'

Then, from the head of the Abbey steps, a man called

out, a figure in green robes. The deep sleeves of his coat, as he raised his arms, were embroidered with zodiacal signs. 'The boy's father was Dragonheaded Uther, his mother Igrayne. It is they who gave him his name – Arthur – and it is they who gave him blood royal enough to rule a nation. Good people, if you wish to see an age of glory and peace, an age to be recorded in letters of gold, bend your knees to Arthur, King of England!'

The common people knelt, but the knights only tossed their crested helmets and swore horribly.

'Do you seriously expect us to walk to heel like puppy dogs because of some wizard's trick and a pretty speech?'

'This is holy ground,' said Merlin. 'No wizardry works on holy ground. Only the magic of Truth.'

The Archbishop, anxious to shift the mob from his gravestones, intoned, 'Come back at Easter! Decide at Easter!'

Above him, Arthur breathed in deeply and said, 'You may come back at Easter and at Whitsun, too. Or next Christmas and every Christmas until Doomsday. However often I pull out the sword, finally each man will have to decide whether I am his king or not. But to every man and woman who does hail me king, I make this pledge. I, Arthur of England shall serve God, defend my country, heal its wounds and lift its heart. I shall uphold justice for all, great or small, rich or poor. By my life, by my honour and by this sword, I swear it!' And he pulled the sword once more from its anvil and held it high, by its blade; the cross-shaped shadow fell like a blessing on the crowd.

A murmur rose to a roar. 'Arthur! We shall have Arthur!'

'None but Arthur for us!'

'Arthur for king!'

The jealous warlords were swept aside by the great goodwill of the ordinary people. Crowds ran through the streets, their dogs and donkeys ran too, boys with barrows, and tradesmen trailing ribbons. Better times were coming. Why not run to meet them?

What opposition Arthur could not overcome by charm and reason, he put down with sword and lance. His seneschal was Sir Kay, his advisor Sir Ector, his teacher Merlin the magician. At his back were soon the best knights in Albion. Together they were invincible.

The Saxon vultures picking over England's bones were suddenly and completely scattered by a pride of lion-hearted knights riding out of the West. And at their head rode Arthur, the true-born king.

Three

THE
SWORD BREAKS

There are five things which make a man a good knight: generosity, fellowship, purity, courtesy and companionship. You may wonder that bravery is not among the knightly virtues. But there are many men who are brave without being good. There are even more brave fools, too foolish to be afraid. The knights who flocked to join King Arthur's court were the best and most virtuous. But they were not the only knights by any means.

One day, while Arthur held court at the castle of Caerleon, news came to him of a knight who had pitched his tent beside the highway and was challenging every man who rode by in armour to fight him or to take some other route. Many, sooner than swallow their pride, agreed to fight him . . . but none of them lived to pass on along the highway. Not after Pellinore camped there.

A young squire called Gryflet begged Arthur on bended knee to be allowed the chance to stop Pellinore's bullying. Kneeling there, with his bright eyes and eager face, Gryflet reminded Arthur so much of himself as a squire that he laid his sword on Gryflet's shoulders and said, 'Arise, bold Sir Gryflet and go adventuring!'

'Was that wise?' whispered Merlin. 'He's scarcely more than a child, and Pellinore is a giant of a man.'

But what was done was done. Arthur could only call after Gryflet, 'Take care, now! Don't be reckless!' Gryflet hardly heard him. He borrowed armour and a horse, lances and a sword, and galloped away to do battle with Pellinore.

Along the highway, beside a bubbling spring, a huge horse was drinking from a pool. A striped pavilion stood there, crowned with a crimson banneret which lolled like a tongue. A row of painted lances were stuck point-down in the earth, and nearby, washed linen hung drying along the branch of a sycamore tree. At the end of the same branch hung Pellinore's shield, its heraldry a clenched fist.

Gryflet rode at the shield and, with his swordhilt, struck it so hard that it fell to the ground. Inside the tent, someone grunted.

When he shouldered his way out of the pavilion,

Pellinore was almost as tall as its crimson banneret, and his hair almost as red. His shoulders were the width of a haycart, and he looked from the fallen shield to Gryflet with a baleful bewilderment. 'What kind of greeting is that from one knight to another?'

'It's a challenge, foul Pellinore!' cried Gryflet in his high, youthful voice. 'A challenge to fight!'

'Fight you? You're no match for me. It would be like wringing chickens. Go home, child.'

Gryflet sidled his horse up against the striped pavilion which promptly collapsed. 'Then shift ground and camp elsewhere, if you won't fight me!'

Pellinore grabbed up his reins and shield and mounted the gigantic horse. 'Since you challenge me, I must fight you,' he bellowed, tugging one of the lances out of the ground, 'but it gives me no satisfaction.' He levelled the lance at Gryflet, told him to defend himself, and came on at the charge.

Gryflet too levelled his lance, but at the last moment he let his shield drop, and Pellinore's long lance entered his body cleanly over the rim. Gryflet fell backwards, though his feet stayed in the stirrups. Lying thus along his horse's rump, face-up to the sun, Sir Gryflet was carried home to Caerleon by his terrified horse.

When Arthur saw him, he was filled with an agony of rage and grief. Without a word, he galloped all the way to Pellinore's camp where he found the huge man still righting his tent. Arthur beat the shield from its branch with the flat of his sword.

'Arm yourself, coward! Murderer of boys! Fight me, if you dare!'

With unhurried movements, almost like weariness, Pellinore mounted and crammed on his helmet. 'Who are you, and what's your quarrel with me?' he asked as he plucked his shield from the tree and a lance from out of the ground.

'I am Arthur, King of England!'

Pellinore's face brightened. 'Ah! I was on my way to offer my sword in your service and to join your company of knights! I only stopped here for a last spell of solitude and contemplation. Let's not fight! I am King Pellinore of—'

'You are the murderer of my knight Gryflet! You showed him as little pity as I shall show you!'

'I regret the lad's death. He had courage,' said Pellinore. 'But he would fight. I meant only to knock him out of the saddle, but in his greenness . . .'

'. . . he died! As you must do now!' Snatching up one of the lances, Arthur rode off to a tourney-distance and turned his horse to charge.

They clashed at full gallop, their lances both striking home. But Pellinore's shield withstood the blow, while Arthur was flung backwards out of the saddle. He rolled to his feet, snatched up a second lance, and remounted.

All the while, Pellinore held off, watching, waiting, courteous. Arthur spurred his horse to a gallop once more, and once more their lances sped home like thrown spears. Both men were unhorsed. Both lances fell in splinters. Arthur drew his sword – the sword-from-the-anvil. The blade of Pellinore's broadsword swung like the paddles of a windmill as he strode towards Arthur; his armour was buckled but his energy unsapped.

No blacksmith's forge ever clanged or clashed with such a din. Blood spurted like sparks from an anvil. To Arthur's dismay and disbelief, Pellinore's blade did not dissolve or shatter as it struck his magic blade. In fact, in the end, Arthur's snapped like an icicle. The broken tip struck him in the thigh, but that did not hurt half so much as knowing he was beaten. Pellinore was six times stronger, his reach longer, his wounds lighter. Arthur was not invincible.

'Yield, my lord, for I have no wish to kill you!'

Arthur wiped the blood out of his eyes and bared his teeth in a sneer. 'I yield to no man! I am Arthur!'

So Pellinore raised his sword to kill the King of Albion.

'Pellinore!' cried a voice out of nowhere.

The huge man tottered – a few steps to the left, a few to the right. His eyes shut, his mouth opened, and he yawned cavernously. Then the weight of his raised sword toppled him backwards into the arms of the sycamore

tree, and he slid down its trunk to the ground, fast asleep amid his laundry.

From behind the tree came Merlin the magician. He stepped unconcernedly over the sleeping giant and came to Arthur's side. Arthur burst into tears.

'What, Merlin, have you killed him? You've cheated him and dishonoured me! He was the rightful victor!'

'King Pellinore is simply sleeping,' said Merlin sharply.

'He was too strong for me. I couldn't . . .'

'King Pellinore is a fine warrior. He will be a great asset among your company of knights,' said Merlin.

'Oh Merlin!' sobbed the King. 'The sword-from-the-anvil! It's broken – smashed! The symbol of my kingship! Is it over, then? My rule? With nothing to show for it?'

'There was no magic in that sword,' said Merlin tersely, 'and if it has served to cut the pride out of your nature, it has done its job well enough. Come with me.'

Despite Arthur's countless injuries, Merlin clearly did not think him about to die, for he bundled him into his saddle and, mounting Pellinore's horse, led Arthur away at a brisk trot into the woods.

They left behind the cultivated fields, the trodden highway, and the open places for the dark green dapple of dense woodland. Though there seemed to be no path, Merlin never once met with bushes or nettles blocking his way. Arthur needed all his strength just to cling to his saddle. The pain seemed one seamless sheath encasing him from head to foot. The trees passed by him in a dizzying palisade.

Just when he thought he must die, they reached a lake – a large, light-luminous lake cradled in the beams of the moon. Mistletoe hung from the boughs over the lake's edge, white like bridal wreaths.

'Announce yourself to the Lady of the Lake,' said Merlin, catching Arthur in his arms as the King slid from his horse. 'Tell her you have come.'

The wonder and mystery of the place filled Arthur with new strength, and although it seemed irreverent to speak aloud in so great a hall of moonlight and water, he stumbled into the shallows and said, 'I am Arthur, King of England.'

'Louder,' said Merlin.

'*I am Arthur, King of England!*' His voice came echoing back to him off banks too distant to be seen.

It was as though a tear had fallen from the face of the moon into the water. For a circle of ripples began to spread out from the very centre of the lake towards the shores. A small boat was moored among the reeds. He knew he must get into it, and no sooner had he done so than it drifted free of its moorings. He paddled with his hands, and his blood made dark birthmarks on the face of the lake. But his eyes were fixed on that single central point from which the ripples were spreading.

As he came close to it, something greenly glimmering, like a serpent's head, broke the surface and pierced the night air. It was the base of a jewelled scabbard. When it rose clear of the water, Arthur could see that it held a sword. For the handguard emerged – wrought and twined from soft gold – and then the hilt, inlaid with precious jewels, bound round with white cords of leather . . . and with fingers of a woman's hand.

The white, smooth, naked arm which brandished the sword in Arthur's face – once, twice, three times – released it gently into his eager hands and shaped itself into a gesture of giving, as if to say, *Take it. It is yours. I have kept it till you came.* Then the hand sank from sight again.

Arthur gazed long and hard into the water, hoping for a glimpse of the Lady of the Lake. But he could see only his own face reflected back at him. 'Thank you,' he whispered.

Some gentle breeze or current, or invisible hand moved the boat gently back towards the reeds. Merlin stood waiting there. 'Some call the sword Caliburn, some Excalibur. Once only in a thousand years is a man born worthy to carry it, and when his work is done, it must be returned to the Lady of the Lake. Guard it well, Arthur. Never be parted from it. Its magic will bring you victory and fame, but its mystery is not in the blade alone.' He put out a hand and helped Arthur ashore, then slid the sheath from Excalibur and touched it – like a green hazel wand – against the raw wounds in Arthur's arms, legs, body and head.

Arthur felt his skin knit, the scars soften, the pain subside, and the strength return to his whole body.

'While you keep this scabbard by you, no wound can kill you, no rope choke you, no poisons steal your breath away. Guard it well, Arthur, and rejoice in Excalibur!'

The ride back to Caerleon did not seem so long to Arthur as the coming had been. When they passed King Pellinore, he was still sleeping. Arthur rode over and touched his many wounds with Excalibur's healing sheath. As they rode away, the huge man began to stir, flicking flies away from his nose.

'Merlin,' said Arthur in as casual a voice as he could

summon. 'Now that the country is at peace, is it not fitting that I . . . ah . . .'

'Yes?' said Merlin sharply.

'. . . that I decide on one castle to be the home of my court?'

Merlin thought for a time and nodded. 'It is fit. Is there one place that pleases you more than another?'

'Camelot,' said Arthur. 'I shall make my court at Camelot.'

They rode a few miles more.

'Merlin . . .' said Arthur hesitantly. 'Now that the country is at peace and I've fixed on a permanent home for my court, is it not fitting that I . . . ah . . .'

'Yes?' snapped Merlin waspishly, and Arthur's courage almost failed him a second time.

'. . . that I marry?'

Merlin thought for a time and nodded. 'It is fit. Is there one lady who pleases you more than another?'

'There is, there is!' Arthur burst out. 'Leodegraunce's daughter. She's the one. There isn't another like her. I've seen her. She's the loveliest . . . It must be her. I'll have no other. It must be Guinevere!'

Merlin was rocked in the saddle as if an arrow had struck him in the chest. Indeed, he put his hand up to his heart.

'Merlin, what is it? What's the matter?'

'Any name but that,' said the magician sorrowfully. 'I

have dreamed this moment, and the future will come of it. Indeed, the end will come of it, the end of Arthur, the end of Camelot, the end of the Golden Age. Unsay it, Arthur.'

But Arthur could not unsay his wish to marry Guinevere. He had seen her and, in seeing, had loved her. And once home, love can no more be pulled harmless out of a man's heart than can the sharp blade of a sword.

Four

THE ROUND TABLE AND THE SORROWFUL BLOW

*M*erlin's wedding gift to Arthur was a table – a circle of wood cut from the largest tree in Albion. It had no head, no foot, and so no places-of-honour ranking one man above another. It was round: as the face is round, as the wheel and the world are round.

Around the table were chairs, and emblazoned on every chairback, in gold, was the name of the knight intended to sit there. Pellinore's name was there, Gawain's and his brother Agravain's, Sir Bedevere's and Sir Bors' – twenty five in all. The lettering was not the work of any earthly goldsmith. In time, some knights died and others came to Camelot and took their place at the Round Table. Then the gold letters would fade, meld, reform and shape themselves into the name of the newcomer.

Only two seats stood empty on the morning of Arthur's wedding. 'One will be filled by your most valiant knight,' said Merlin, 'the King's own champion, who is not yet come to Camelot. The other is the Seat of Mortal Danger. If any man sits in this, without the merit to do so, ravens will mob him and the fiery breath of dragons devour him. Only the purest and most perfect of all men shall take his place there.'

So for all its roundness, there *were* seats of honour at the Round Table.

Some, out of curiosity or envy, tested the unnamed seat. But no one dared to sit in the Seat of Mortal Danger. Not even Balin or Balan.

Balin and Balan were, at that time, the greatest of the knights at King Arthur's court. They were twins – as like as two fists – and were utterly inseparable. Like the two white knights on a chess board, they rode through the vales of Albion side by side.

One day a lady came on foot to Camelot. She came out of the forest where Arthur had received Excalibur – a long enough walk, heaven knows. But the great broadsword dragging from her belt must have made it seem ten times as far. 'Is there a knight here good and true enough to take this sword out of its scabbard?' she asked the assembled court.

Everyone tried and everyone failed – even Arthur, to his great surprise. Then Balin stepped up, and the sword slid from its scabbard as smoothly as the sword from the anvil or Excalibur from the lake. The young woman looked him up and down admiringly.

Balin and Balan came from humble beginnings; they barely had the means to arm and clothe themselves. So Balin said, weighing the weapon in his hand, 'I have one sword, but nothing so fine as this. I'll keep this for ever and a day.'

The maiden burst into such a storm of tears that Balin's brother intervened. 'Now see, brother. She didn't mean you to keep it. Give her back the sword!'

'It is not for myself that I weep,' said the maiden. 'It is for Balin.' And she turned away, letting the scabbard slide from among the folds of her lake-green skirts.

From that day on, Balin wore two swords. Even when he laid them aside to sleep, he still wore the name of Knight-with-Two-Swords. It was the first way in which he had ever differed from Balan.

Word came to Camelot of a knight called Garlon, who was without one speck of honour, without one virtuous hair to his head. Balin went questing after this savage villain. He went alone, without Balan, for now he thought of himself as the Knight-with-Two-Swords and not as his brother's twin.

His quest carried him into the neighbouring lands of King Pelles, to the home of a rich gentleman. The house was full of crying, for the gentleman's only son lay wounded and in agony on his brocade-and-velvet bed.

'Three days ago I jousted with Garlon – the King's brother – at Corbenic Castle,' the father explained. 'God was with me the day of the joust – or so I thought. I unhorsed Garlon twice. But his pride was so wounded by losing, that he turned on my poor unarmed boy and cut him down out of sheer spite. Here's the spear he did it with. Now nothing can save my son but the blood of the knight who wounded him.' The father's eyes filled with tears as he looked down at his beloved boy.

Then Balin swore, by his two swords, to fetch the old man the medicine his son needed – Sir Garlon's blood. And taking the shaft of the broken spear with him, he continued his quest, knowing his destination now. He must find Corbenic Castle, home of King Pelles and Garlon.

From the moment it came into view, Balin knew Corbenic was no castle grubbed up out of English quarries. Its walls were too white, its banners too bright, the flowers in its moat too deep-drifted. There was birdsong without birds, and the sound of a banquet in progress.

When he knocked at the gate, he was made as welcome as if it were his own home. It was a feast day, and he was invited to join the festivities. The squires gave him soft, rich clothes instead of his armour, and offered to store his swords safely.

'No! I never part with my swords,' said Balin hurriedly.

When he went in to dinner, he scrutinized the guests one by one for a glimpse of the villainous Garlon. Delightful music was playing. Pelles called Balin to sit beside him and they began to talk. The King seemed to be everything Balin had heard of him: courteous, generous and wise. Balin continued to look about him at the other guests. But the food was piled so high on the table, that it was difficult to see every face. Suddenly a hand removed a roast duck and there, in the space, cramming duck-meat into his mouth, was a face Balin knew without introduction. The cheeks were purple-black with broken veins, the eyes red-lidded and treacherous.

'Who do you think you're staring at?' demanded Garlon, spattering Balin with half-chewed meat.

What was Balin to do? He was a guest under King Pelles' roof. All the laws of hospitality forbad him to draw a sword here. And yet he had sworn! Balin hesitated.

'Eat your meat, worm, and drink your ale. It's what you came for, isn't it?' snarled Garlon.

'Brother, please—' Pelles began. 'Can you never be civil?' But Balin had reached a decision. He would not draw his sword. He would use the very spear with which Garlon had hurt the little boy. Calmly he confronted Garlon:

'This is the spear you used to kill many a good knight and to harm a child. I did not come here to eat or drink, no, but to return your spear!' And with that he sank it into Garlon's great belly.

Mayhem broke loose then. Knights lunged at Balin with fists and eating knives. Balin drew his sword, and prepared to defend himself.

'Fiend! You've killed my brother!' roared King Pelles. 'I'll have your life for that!'

'Try and take it!' replied Balin, unrepentant.

Pelles grabbed up from the table a fearful meat cleaver. The first blow smashed the spear shaft in Balin's hand. The second his marvellous sword. Balin took to his heels and fled – out of the hall, down passageways and stairwells, through chambers and anterooms, darting ahead of the furious, grief-stricken king. There was no breath to spare for explanations: Balin simply ran.

Acre upon acre of flagged floors stretched away, like a great chessboard. He pushed his way past wall hangings and bed curtains, through cellars and lofts, through fireplaces and cupboards, and always there were more rooms beyond – a maze of rooms and hallways.

At last he ran up a spiral stair, on and on till his legs were fire under him, and emerged into a bedroom. Quiet fell over him like a thick mattress; it winded him. A gilded bed stood against the wall under a canopy of gold. Someone was lying in the bed, someone so old and frail that his skin was almost transparent. A spear stood propped against the wall, a spear of solid gold.

At his back, Balin heard running on the stairs, then the whistle of the meat cleaver. To defend himself, Balin grabbed up the golden spear and turned. King Pelles ran directly on to its shining point and, in that second, the man in the bed sat up with a cry.

Darkness filled the room like smoke. Time lurched. The wind blew backwards. King Pelles grabbed at his thigh and wrested the spear from the wound, but the gash was deep and terrible. Pelles fell.

So too did his castle.

Turrets teetered and toppled, crashing through the roof. The wall in front of Balin's face melted into a hole, the hole yawned, the countryside beyond was bleached white. A whirlwind of stonedust pulverized the cattle in the valley, shredded the leaves from the trees and felled every byre and sheepfold for miles around. A howling wind buffeted Balin about and about, the golden bedclothes wound him round. The floor under his feet collapsed, and he seemed to fall as far as Hell itself amid rubble and the remnants of the feast.

Across four counties the wind blew. Every house in its path fell, like sandcastles in a rising tide. The wind seared all greenness to brown and turned all water to gall. Trees lay down, baring blackened roots. Birds fell from the sky like rain.

For three days Balin lay in the rubble of Corbenic Castle. All the while he lay there, he could hear the King crying out for someone to ease his pain. Crows hopped over the ruins during daylight. Foxes brushed by in the dark.

Then Merlin came.

He unearthed Balin, as a gypsy unearths hedgehogs from the ashes of a fire. But he showed small joy in finding him. 'That was a sorrowful blow you struck, Balin. Four counties were laid waste when you wounded the good King Pelles.'

'Help him, then! Cure him with your magic, Merlin! I didn't mean . . .'

'Nothing can heal the wound you struck. You made it with the Spear of the Centurion, you see. That spear pierced the side of Christ Jesus as He hung dying on the Cross.'

'And the man in the bed? Who was that?'

'His name,' said Merlin, 'is beyond your imagining. But I tell you, Balin, only the blood of Christ Himself can heal King Pelles' wound.'

Blood to heal a wound. At that, Balin remembered his

quest, and opened his cupped hand. Lying in the palm was the blood of Garlon, dried to a red dust. 'Help me reach the boy Garlon wounded,' he begged Merlin. 'Then I am ready to face whatever punishment God sends.'

Through grey landscapes of desolation they rode, amid trees turned to stone and whole herds of cattle bones. The house of the rich gentleman was riven with cracks, and holes gaped in its roof. But the wounded boy still lay on his brocade-and-velvet bed; his father still wept over him.

Balin spilled the dried blood of Garlon into the boy's terrible wound. At once the child began to recover. There, amid devastation, father and son embraced.

'Will anyone ever do the same for good King Pelles?' Balin asked Merlin.

'I have dreamed of a quest to find Christ's holy blood,' said Merlin, 'and the future will come of my dream. But neither you nor I shall live to see it.'

They parted company there, with hardly a kind word. Merlin took the smashed sword and rode back to Camelot, to tell of the ruin which had overtaken four counties. Balin rode on.

Balin rode until he came to a castle untouched by the catastrophe of the Sorrowful Stroke. He was utterly exhausted, and his two scabbards clashed together at his side and scared the birds out of the trees. He did not realize that he had come to the castle of Morgan le Fay.

When he knocked on the castle gate, a woman, veiled in green, called down to him from the ramparts. 'Before you enter, you must fight the champion of the castle. It is the custom.'

'Must I? I'm fearfully tired,' said Balin. But the woman smiled so encouragingly; she even came down to him with a suit of armour, and took the battered shield from his arm – the one with his crest upon it. 'Look the thongs are nearly frayed through, you must have another. Courage, friend. You need only exchange a blow or two – just so that custom is served.'

Morgan le Fay returned indoors. At her dining table sat another knight who had arrived earlier in the day. He was just finishing the meal she had prepared for him when she went and knelt by his chair and wrung his hand pleadingly.

'Please help me! A stranger is at the gate, and I'm frightened! He's just destroyed four counties with his wickedness. Defend me from him, I beg you, dear, *dear* Balan. You will? Then you shall carry a shield with my very own crest on it, to show you are fighting on my behalf! Oh thank you!'

That is how Balan came face-to-face with Balin his brother, and neither knew it, because Morgan had made sure neither was carrying his own shield. Balan even saw the two scabbards at Balin's waist and recalled, with a pang of sorrow, the Knight-with-Two-Swords. But he did not for one moment imagine that the helmeted stranger with the uncrested shield was his own twin brother.

As twins they were evenly matched, of course. In strength, in daring, in stamina there was not the smallest difference between them. Balan attacked with fury – no friendly clash of swords, this – and Balin retaliated. They fought on and on, like a man and his reflection, matching blow for blow, wound for wound, pain for pain.

At last, when every shred of armour had been hacked away and their faces were masked with blood, they fell to their knees, too exhausted to fight on, too exhausted for their hearts to beat above ten times more.

'Who are you?' panted Balan. 'I never met my match before.'

'I am Balin, and God knows, I met my match in you!'

Then Balan gave a terrible cry. '*Balin? Where was your shield? Where was your crest? Do you think I would have killed my own brother if I had known it was you?*'

The twins wept on each other's faces, until the blood was washed away. Then they died in each other's arms . . . just as Morgan le Fay had intended them to do. In Camelot's great hall, the golden letters faded from two of the seats at the Round Table.

The vengeful Morgan, half-sister to Arthur, came out of the castle gate, and laid the knights' own shields over them, laughing.

'And now for you, Merlin,' she said under her breath.

Merlin, meanwhile, mended Balin's broken sword – the one the maiden had brought – and sank it in a massive block of red marble. The block he floated on the river – floated it, yes, as though it were a wooden boat and mast, not marble run through with iron.

It turned on the eddies, paused in the backwaters, languished long summers tangled in the mare's-tail weed. But little by little, it floated downstream, downstream towards Camelot.

Five

BURIED ALIVE

She came out of the forest – from the direction of the Lake, or perhaps from the Land of Faeries beyond. She was beautiful, in a wild, bewitching way. Her beauty caught the eye. Her orange silken robe caught one man's eye like a flame, and her name scorched itself on his heart in letters of gold: *Nimue*.

It was not Arthur, nor one of his hot-blooded knights. To everyone's amusement and astonishment, it was *Merlin* who fell in love with Nimue. From the first moment he saw her, he was consumed with longing.

'Merlin! You? With your wise words and your deep thoughts? I thought you were proof against these things!' Arthur joked.

Merlin did not smile. 'No man is proof against his Fate. When I see her, I can't breathe. She will steal my breath from me, as sure as Eve gave the world to the Devil.'

'You mean you know she'll do you harm? Then magic yourself out of love! Just stop loving . . .' But his words petered away. For he recalled how Merlin had once told him to stop loving Guinevere, and he knew how impossible it had been to obey. Besides, Merlin was not listening.

Wherever Nimue went, Merlin followed her. Like a magnet she drew him. She asked him to go away, but it was not in his power to go. Like a man who has tasted seawater, his thirst for her grew more burning all the while, and his good sense crumbled into madness.

So she asked him to teach her his magic, and he did, spilling secrets into her lap that he had never shared with anyone. She sucked all his magical honey. But she did not, could not or would not love Merlin in return.

Sensing his own future, Merlin tried to warn Arthur of his. 'Beware, my lord! Keep your sword with you always! Sleep with your scabbard by your side! Soon I won't be here to help you. Beware, in time, of Sir Lance—'

'Not here? Why, are you going somewhere, Merlin?' asked Arthur.

'To my grave. Into a grave. Out of the light,' said Merlin, his face a picture of torment. 'Buried alive. I have dreamed it, and the future will come of my dreams.'

'Oh but Merlin, surely you're the one man in Albion who doesn't need to fear the future! If you see danger coming, you can avoid it!'

But Merlin looked back at him like a swimmer on an ebb tide, carried farther and farther out to sea.

Desperate for new ways to express his love, Merlin told Nimue the most romantic love story he knew – of Anasteu and Ester: ' . . . His father forbad them to marry. So the lovers ran away into the forest and lived there as wild and free as the deer. Prince Anasteu carved a room from a crude woodland cave, and hung it with carpets and pictures – his Palace of Love. – I could show you the place; it's quite close by. – Their love lasted as long as their lives, and on the day one died, well so did the other. Because they were all in all to each other, you see. The cave was sealed up as their tomb.'

When Merlin finished, he was flustered to see Nimue gazing at him intently. 'What it would be to be loved like that!' she sighed.

Merlin's heart thudded. 'Oh but I—'

'Could you really? Could you really show me the cave?'

'We'll go right away, if you want.'

Together they rode out of Camelot and into the greenwood. Merlin could barely believe his good fortune, to have Nimue all to himself, to have her talking of love rather than magic. Here perhaps, he could make her believe the length and depth of his love.

'This is the place – the Cave of the Lovers,' he said as they reined in beside a huge rock smothered in ivy and moss. 'They died in each other's arms, at the same instant, or so the story goes. They say no one ever loved as they loved, but Nimue, oh Nimue, I—'

'Show me.'

'What?'

'Show me the bodies of the lovers. Move the stone away and let me see them wrapped in each other's arms. Oh do, please!'

'But they've been dead a hundred years, lady . . .'

'I'd give anything to see them,' murmured Nimue pleadingly, her smile sweeter than ever before.

So Merlin used his magic to move the giant stone sealing the Lovers' Cave. Like Easter morning, the cave-room appeared before them.

There lay the legendary lovers, wrapped in each other's arms. The maiden was as perfectly beautiful as on the day she died, the prince as perfectly handsome. Death's decay had been held off by their great love, like a wolf kept at bay by firelight.

'I shall sleep here tonight,' declared Nimue.

'Oh but . . .' Merlin stifled his objections. The love permeating this place might infect Nimue. In the morning he would urge her to marry him – promise her her own Cave of Love and everlasting adoration. 'I'll stay here to protect you from the dangers of the forest,' he said, and she did not object. She did not send him away!

They made up two beds, side by side, in the Cave of

Love. The white marble walls sweated silver moisture, and sweat broke from Merlin's brow, too. The place was heady with century-old perfumes; they made his head swim. Nimue unfastened her hair, and Merlin felt his blood cascade through his heart like a waterfall. Nimue let her orange robe fall to the ground . . . and Merlin fell too, fainting under the burden of too much love.

He fell on to one of the beds, and Nimue covered him with his cloak. She dressed again and lit a fire. Then taking potions and liquors from his saddle panniers, and the words he had taught her, she laid a great enchantment on Merlin.

'I have to be free of you, you see,' Nimue whispered. 'You clung to me closer than convolvulus. You suffocated me with your love, like a pillow pressed over my face. You would have buried me alive in your love, if you could – smothered me with your loving. That's why I must bury you here, with only your dreams for company. Farewell, magical Merlin. If only I *could* have loved you, what a pair we would have made, you and I.'

Merlin sank into a world of dreams. As Nimue stepped out of the cave, he moaned in his sleep:

'Oh Arthur, beware of Morgan le Fay! Beware!'

By the magic she had learned from Merlin, Nimue sealed the cave, mounted her horse and drove Merlin's away into the wood. At last she was free of him.

But they worried her, those last words of his. She felt

a weight settle on her shoulders, and could not shake it off. What was this danger from Morgan le Fay? Why would Arthur's own sister wish him harm? Nimue had already taken her magic from Merlin; now she realized she had also taken on his duty: to worry and care for the King in a dark and dangerous world.

Six

THE
FAERY SHIP

M organ le Fay had a husband called Uriens. But she loved another man, Sir Accolon. Neither was a wicked man; they did not share her hatred of Arthur. Indeed, they visited him at Camelot, and hunted with him in the great greenwood.

As the royal hunting party chased a stag one day, Arthur, Uriens and Accolon outrode the rest, and found themselves on the bank of a broad river. Moving against the current, a large ship came upriver towards them. Its wooden walls were draped with red silk right down to the waterline. When it hove-to, a gangplank was lowered to touch the bank at their feet. The knights could see no crew but for twelve beautiful women, their hands clasped and hidden prayerfully within their sleeves.

'Come aboard, sirs, and take some refreshment,' said

one. 'You must be weary from the hunt.'

Such was the magic and strangeness of the world in those days, that all three went cheerfully aboard. They found themselves in a place more palace than ship, with bowls of warm water to wash in, and new robes laid ready for them to wear. They were brought food and scarlet wine. Perfumed tapers gave off tufts of sweet white smoke.

Soon the rigours of the day and the splendour of the evening made Arthur, Uriens and Accolon sleepy. They were shown to individual cabins, to beds as soft as swansdown, and rocked to sleep by the motion of the moored boat.

When Uriens awoke, he was in his own bed. His wife Morgan lay on her back beside him, her eyelids tight closed and a smile on her lips. She stirred at once when he cried out. 'I was on . . . I dreamt I . . . !' Uriens fingered the shirt he was wearing: it was clean and soft and unfamiliar. But Morgan seemed to find nothing strange in how he looked or how he came to be there. So he concluded it must have been a dream, a white-sailed dream. But where, then, were Arthur and Accolon?

Sir Accolon awoke in a field, his cloak over his face and his armour heaped beside him in a cairn. His horse was tethered to a nearby tree. He fingered his robes, new and

clean and unfamiliar. At his feet stood a sword, its tip rammed into the ground; he of course assumed it was his, and put it on. Someone was walking towards him across the field; he would ask her for directions to Camelot. The faery ship must have been a vision, he concluded, a white-sailed vision. But where, then, were Arthur and Uriens?

Arthur awoke in a castle dungeon. He still wore the robes given him aboard the faery ship, but a rat was curled up asleep in the fur hem. Where were Accolon and Uriens?

The door opened, and a woman entered. She began to answer his questions before he had even asked them.

'This castle belongs to Sir Damas. He needs a champion to fight in his name, for he bears the scars of many a battle and cannot fight himself. Will you fight for him?'

Arthur was feeling a fool for being so easily taken prisoner. 'Who must I fight?' he asked.

'Damas's brother, Sir Ontzlake. Their feud is long and bitter. You may end it and win your freedom at the same time.'

'You may tell Sir Damas that if he will return my sword to me, I shall fight on his behalf.'

The woman immediately brought Arthur his sword: it had the weight, the shine, the shape of Excalibur. So

Arthur took the field full of confidence, knowing that he must be better armed than his foe.

There was something familiar about the rider who came towards him over the castle's greensward. It was not the livery, for the livery he had never seen. It was not the face, for his face, like Arthur's, was hidden behind a visor. But the bulk and build of the man were somehow familiar, even so.

They fought like demons, hacking and slashing, boring and barging till their horses fell dead beneath them, and their armour buckled. From the very first blow Arthur knew something was wrong, for his sword did not slice through steel nor cut sparks out of the air, whereas his own armour was being hacked away, like the peel off an apple. Soon the sword in his hands was chipped and bent and bowed, his body cut to the bone by a hundred blows.

'Yield, man!' cried the stranger. 'You bleed!'

'I'd as soon eat dirt and die as yield,' said Arthur. But at the next blow, his sword broke off at the hilt, a useless stub, a counterfeit. He knew that the *real* Excalibur was in the hands of his opponent.

Ontzlake came on, slashing and jabbing, his jewelled scabbard swinging. 'Yield, for God's sake, before I kill you!'

'Never fear. I have no plans to die yet!' With a massive effort, Arthur struck out with his shield. He knocked

Ontzlake off his feet and the sword out of his hand. The hilt felt as comfortable in Arthur's palm as the handshake of a friend – 'You have been away too long, Excalibur!' – and thinking this stranger must have robbed him, he pounded on him like a blackbird on a snail. He sliced the jewelled scabbard away; after that, every blow Arthur inflicted left a gaping wound. At last, the stranger's visor spun away into the bushes.

'*Accolon*!'

'Who calls me by my name?' asked Accolon, falling to his knees. 'Who has killed me and knows my name?'

Arthur lifted his bevor to look at Sir Accolon. 'I am Arthur, King of Albion.'

Accolon's blood soaked the grass. 'Oh my lord! I never knew! I see now! It was Morgan my lover – Morgan your sister – Morgan le Fay! She set me on you like her dog! She hates you so bitterly. A thousand times she begged me to murder you, but I always refused. Kill my King? Murder my friend? Not even for love of a lady! But yesterday, as I lay in a field, fuddled with sleep, a veiled woman came to me and spun me a tale of feuding brothers. "Fight this tyrant Damas," she said, and set this sword in my hand and this scabbard by my side. I mistook them for my own. I see now, this was Morgan's doing.'

The faery magic was falling from their eyes like tears now. It seemed impossible that they should not have known their own swords, not recognized each other. There was no Ontzlake, no Damas: only the conniving of faeries and the malice of Morgan.

'I forgive you, Accolon,' said Arthur, 'and my heart bleeds for you.' As Arthur strapped on the scabbard of Excalibur, his wounds closed. But Accolon died within the hour.

Too weak to travel home, Arthur sent for aid, and when his knights arrived, they carried him to a nearby convent to recuperate. But he would not rest until he had given one last command. 'Send the body of Accolon to my sister, and tell her, "This is what your treachery has bought you: a dead lover and a world of shame." '

When Morgan le Fay saw the man she loved, face-down across his horse, her face turned deathly pale, but she hid it with her hair.

'Your brother Arthur sends you back the body of your lover, Sir Accolon,' said the messenger loud and clear, for everyone to hear. 'He says, "This is what your treachery has bought you: a dead lover and a world of shame." '

Morgan's husband Uriens was aghast. 'Is this true, Morgan?'

But when the cascade of black hair fell back from her face, she was laughing. 'Tell my brother: enough of his jokes! Lover indeed! Ha ha!' She laughed it off. She laughed so loud and long that everyone else started laughing too. A joke, yes. 'How is my *dear* brother?'

'His life hangs by a thread, lady. He is resting and recuperating at a convent near where he fought Sir Accolon.'

'I am very sorry to hear it,' said Morgan.

And truly she was, for only news of Arthur's death could have brought her any joy at that moment. That night, she left home on horseback, with her bodyguard of mounted men. She rode north through the Waste Land.

The knights guarding the gates to the convent stood half asleep. Her silent approach startled and flustered them. They peered into the dark hollow of her hood and saw the Lady Morgan's eyes glare out at them, ferocious and determined. They fell back, they stammered in confusion: 'No visitors, ma'am! The King said . . . We were told . . .'

'Out of my way!' Morgan told them. 'Am I not his sister?' She swept by them, a rattle of purple samite and black wool, her face as white as the scarf circling it. She swept majestically along the low corridors to the door of a cell.

There, on the bed, lay Arthur, sleeping. But even in sleep his hand was closed round the hilt of Excalibur. She could not steal that without waking him. But the jewelled scabbard was a different matter. She had only to slide it off the blade. Its inlaid jewels flashed green as envy as her hand closed round it. Arthur stirred in his sleep.

Tucking the scabbard under her cloak, Morgan slipped back along the bare white corridors and out past the guard. If a panther had stalked by them, their hair might have stood on end in much the same way.

Seven

MORGAN'S GIFT

*T*he noise of horses galloping away woke Arthur. His opening eyes saw Excalibur. His waking hand groped about for the scabbard which had brought such magic healing to his wounds.

It was gone.

'Who has been here?' His voice rang down the white corridor.

'Only your sister, sire. No one but your sister!'

They went after Morgan – a troop of knights raising a cloud of dust and a noise like thunder.

'Someone is following fast, lady,' said Morgan's outrider. 'Twenty or thirty men in armour.'

Morgan and her bodyguard were just then skirting the shore of a large pond, deep and fetid and aswarm with hatching flies. Morgan took the scabbard from under her cloak. 'If I may not have you, he shan't!' she cried.

One, twice, three times she whirled the leather sheath above her head – a blur of glittering colours. Then she flung it out into deep water where it sank down, down into oozing mud. It is lying there now, gem-studded afresh with water-snails, its magic healing the fishes of all their wounds.

Morgan rode on at full speed, but Arthur and his knights rode faster. The distance between them closed with every passing mile. At last the chase brought them to a bare valley strewn with boulders, walled with beetling cliffs. Morgan reined in her horse and turned her face to the sky. She began to speak magic, to chant on a single note. The horses shifted uneasily, wagging their heads, feeling the air grow cold. The soldiers, too, shivered.

'Feli meli svoigam grimlach
Feli meli brinwort eis strees.
Cyl enemyll, cyl Arturi:
Transyv mem in cymti gris:
Hyden meme lessen blach.'

A strange silence settled over the company of horsemen and their commander. Their bridles ceased to jingle, their stirrups to swing. The horses turned as grey as dusk. The men's beards stiffened, their features set, and their backbones turned, vertebra by vertebra, into columns of pebbles balanced one on another. In short, they turned to stone, their breath to dust, and their outline against the cliff to no more than the fresco carving on a wall. At their head stood the 'statue' of Morgan, her robe grey, her horse grey, her skin and bone grey over grey.

Entering the valley, Arthur's horse slowed to a halt, trembling violently. The King dismounted and ran his fingers over the contours of flank and mane and robe. He stood before the 'carving' of his sister and gazed up at her stony features, beautiful, hard, bloodless, believing all life had gone out of her. Either she had put this terrible end to herself, out of guilt, or else her magic had soured into this paralysing greyness. He laid his hand over hers – a stone hand resting on a stone pommel. Then he turned away, with tears in his eyes. 'Mount up, men,' he said, 'and let's go home.'

After he had gone, after the noise of galloping had faded to silence, the rock face shivered. Puffs of dust erupted here and there, and pebbles trickled down. With the slowness of sap returning to a winter tree, Morgan's hand turned from grey to pink then lifted from the pommel of her saddle. She raised it in a triumphant fist. Behind her, the dozen stone horses shook themselves and broke free of the cliff, bridles jingling, nostrils snorting.

That bulging rockface struck such horror and sadness into Arthur that when word came that his sister was still alive, he was almost glad. The news came in the shape of a pretty girl. She came from the direction of the forest.

Across both her arms hung a cloak of rich green, embroidered from collar to hem with the 'eyes' of peacock-feathers; their oily iridescence caught the light. The girl knelt down beside Arthur's wooden seat and smiled sweetly up at him.

'My mistress is so very sorry for the wrong she has done you and the hate she has shown you. She longs to mend what is broken between you. And to make amends, she sends this cloak, a gift from a loving, repentant sister.'

The beautiful cloak was laid on the Round Table. The feathers' herls lifted in the draught from the open door.

'I welcome my sister's love,' said Arthur. 'But won't you show me this marvellous cloak? Be my mirror. Show me how it looks around a pair of shoulders.'

The messenger swayed on her knees. 'You are a tall man, sire, and I hardly as tall as your elbow. The cloak would swamp me.'

'Never mind. Show it me, even so,' said Arthur. 'Put it on.'

'It was made for a king, sire. Not for the likes of me.' Her face had turned very white, her lids drawn back very wide. When she steadied herself against his chair, her hand left a sweat-dark mark.

Arthur did not lose his temper. He simply insisted. 'You shall wear it, my dear. Stand up and let me help you on with it.'

With a flourish of green and purple iridescence, Arthur swung the cloak around the messenger's shoulders. She screamed and tried to run, but the feather-light folds settled around her.

As Arthur fastened the clasp at her throat, he had to snatch away his hands, to save them from being burnt. For a column of fire erupted, like a volcano's lava: a geyser of liquid fire. It leapt upwards and scorched the roof timbers. It scorched the faces of the knights of the Round Table. It sprinkled the table with black, feathery ash. When the fire was out, no more remained of either cloak or messenger than a sickening smell.

'So this is the present my sister sends me to mend the rift between us,' said Arthur. 'From this moment forward, Morgan le Fay is my sworn enemy. Let her not step inside my kingdom and live.'

Morgan, hearing how her murderous plot had failed, stamped her foot among the forest's leafmould so that all the little worms in the ground trembled and died.

Eight

GREEN

The feast of Christmas lasted a week. The damp dank of winter was driven back with bonfires and music, and the knights and ladies at Camelot danced and feasted day by night by morning. King Arthur and Queen Guinevere sat on a platform hung with bright banners and swags of silk, while storytellers told tales of brave deeds and magic. Outside, the world was grey and bare and dead, the ground so hard with frost that it seemed impossible spring would ever again break through, green. But by New Year's day at Camelot, the outside world was forgotten in favour of firelight and smoke, singing and wine.

Suddenly the great doors, armoured with frost, swung open, and in came a man on horseback, ducking his head beneath the keystone of the arch. The clatter of hooves alone would have caught everyone's attention. But the rider himself made the Round Table knights stare. For he was a giant of a man, as tall as a tree, with hands as gnarled as roots and hair matted with leaves. He must have ridden through woodland, for strands of ivy wound his body round, and twigs of holly were caught in his clothing. There seemed to be birds or martins in his pockets. And he was green.

The man was green: his hair, his hands, his matted beard, his face, were all green. Even his horse was green, and the huge axe which hung from his saddle and swung to and fro, to and fro.

'Greetings to the court of Camelot,' boomed the giant. 'Your fame has spread far.'

Arthur gave a start and remembered his manners. 'You are welcome, stranger, to join our feast.'

'Oh but I'm not here for meat and wine,' said the Green Knight. 'I heard that the knights of Arthur were the bravest alive, and I have come to deliver a challenge.'

Arthur swallowed hard. 'A challenge? To single combat, you mean? Your challenge shall be answered. I or one of my knights . . .'

'Not combat, no!' said the giant, laughing. 'Am I a bully to pick quarrels with men half my size? No, my quest is to find a man with courage enough to trade me blow for blow. He shall strike me one blow with this axe of mine. Then I shall strike him back!'

Silence filled the room. He was such a jolly, grinning man that no one there wished him any harm at all. It is one thing to hurt a man in the heat of battle, but another to hit him with an axe, on New Year's day, in front of a cosy fire.

'Shame, shame. I see you are all cowards, after all,' said the Green Knight sadly. He made as if to remount his horse.

At that, Sir Gawain jumped up – Arthur's own nephew. 'I will answer your challenge!' he said, and the Green Knight turned on him a beaming, green smile.

'Good lad. Excellent lad. Here! I shall bend down for you, or you will never reach high enough.' So saying, he knelt down, swept his long green hair forward over his head, and laid bare his long green neck. It looked like a mossy bough of oak.

Gawain began to regret his rashness. This did not seem a very brave and knightly deed – to strike an unarmed man – even if he was green. But Gawain realized that if he could just kill the knight with one blow, then he would not have to suffer a blow himself, from that appalling axe.

So he swung the blade high, and he swung it hard. The ladies covered their eyes. The axe fell, and the green neck was sliced right through.

Like fruit from a tree, the head fell with a thud and rolled across the floor. Crimson blood splashed Gawain. A flurry of snow blew in at the open door. Everyone felt rather sorry.

Then the Green Knight drew in his arms and legs, and got slowly to his feet.

Gawain felt his stomach turn to water; he had just forfeited his life. Now it was his turn to lose his head. The Green Knight went lumbering after his head. He retrieved it from under a bench, and held it in one hand, by its long, green hair. The mouth was still smiling that broad, green smile. Then it spoke:

> *'Well struck, Gawain, your blade was true.*
> *Now may I do the same to you.*
> *Your one blow I may now repay . . .*
> *But not until next New Year's day.*
> *One year from now, search out my home:*
> *To the Green Chapel come – alone,*
> *Or all the knights assembled here*
> *Shall call you "Coward!" Until next year!'*

Mounting his horse, the headless green giant rode out through the open door. This time he did not need to duck his head, which was tucked securely under one arm, whistling softly as it dripped blood on to the green horse. There was a Christmassy look, scarlet and green, about the departing giant.

Gawain, still holding the axe, looked around him at his fellow knights. No one said, 'Don't go.' No one said, 'That was unfair.' Gawain had accepted a knightly challenge, and he was bound to keep his rendezvous at the Green Chapel next New Year's day.

The sun recovered its heat and thawed the winter world. Green shoots pierced the mail-hard ground. It was spring.

The moon waxed and waned, the April storms blew themselves blue in the face. Crops ripened in the fields. It was summer.

The trees blazed with colour. The berries blushed. The birds migrated towards the sun, the golden leaves towards the ground. It was autumn.

And Sir Gawain, unable to put off his journey another day, set off in search of the Green Chapel. He had no idea where it was, or how to find it. So he asked wherever he went, 'Do you know of a place called the Green Chapel or a giant of a knight, all green?' But no one did.

Wolves and bears attacked him. Giants and trolls, bandits and monsters chased him through thorny dens and bleak heaths. He asked as he fought them, 'Do you know of a place called the Green Chapel or a giant of a knight, all green?' But he came away with only his life, and another nick in his sword.

He rescued children from drowning, and ladies from captivity, deer from snares and men from flagpoles. And he asked, as he rescued them, 'Do you know of a place called the Green Chapel or a giant of a knight, all green?'

But he came away with only their thanks (or a grateful kiss from the ladies).

He rode through raw winds and blizzards of falling leaves, through frozen bracken and driving rain. He began to think that he would never find the Green Chapel by New Year, and that he would be branded a coward for not keeping his appointment. But when it began to hail, he hardly cared any more. The pellets of ice hammered dents in his armour, and he began to change colour himself – not to green, but to a goosey blue, with a red nose and red finger-ends.

Seeing a castle, he vowed to sleep indoors that night. It was Christmas Eve, after all.

The owner of the house greeted him like an old friend. 'Come in! Sit down! Eat! Drink! Warm yourself! Stay the night! Stay twenty! You look exhausted. Let me find you a dry suit of clothes.'

'A bed would be as sweet to me as to Mary in Bethlehem on the first Christmas Eve,' said Gawain. 'But I can't stay. I am looking for the Green Chapel and the green giant who lives there. I must find it by New Year's day.'

'Then you shall stay a week!' exclaimed his host. 'For the Green Chapel stands only two miles from here.'

Sir Gawain's heart shrank inside him. He would keep his rendezvous and never live to see another spring. It could not be helped. At least his last days need not be spent out in the wet and cold. Gawain resigned himself and accepted his host's invitation.

The man's name was Sir Bertilak, and he had a lovely wife, Fidelia. Long after the meal was eaten, the chess played, the wine drunk, Fidelia would keep Gawain enthralled with her charming chatter and ready wit. She clearly found Gawain charming, too, for she scarcely took her eyes off him.

Two days after Christmas, the weather improved, and Bertilak decided to go hunting. 'I can see you're still too weary from your journey to come with me,' he said. 'You stay and take life easy: my wife will look after you. Tell you what! At the end of each day, I shall give you what I've taken in the hunt, and you shall give me whatever the day has brought you! Agreed?'

'With all my heart,' said Gawain.

Next day, Sir Bertilak went hunting, and Gawain lay in his bed scribbling. He would give his host a poem he had decided, in exchange for whatever he hunted: the last poem of his life. So how should it go?

The poem was never finished. Fidelia put her head round the door and smiled a dazzling smile. 'Well? And how is handsome Gawain, hero of my heart?' She came and sat on the bed. Gawain drew the covers up to his chin. 'They say you are a great wooer of ladies,' she whispered. 'Won't you show me, while my husband is out?'

'I don't know who told you such a thing,' said Gawain, blushing deeply. 'I'm a true knight, and a pure knight would never be so bold with a married lady.'

But Fidelia would not go away. She wanted to be kissed by the famous Gawain. Apparently his kisses were famous, even in this remote backwater of the world. She was an uncommonly pretty lady. But Gawain could think only of New Year's day. He very much wanted to go to Heaven when he died, so he had no intention of behaving badly. There again, he did not like to offend the lady . . .

In the end, he decided one kiss would do no harm, and he let Fidelia kiss him. It was rather like being licked by a cat.

When Sir Bertilak came home, he had caught nothing but a mangy old fox. Still, he gave it to Gawain according to their bargain. Gawain took a deep breath. 'Then I must keep my side of the bargain, too,' he said, and grasping Bertilak by the shoulders, he planted a big kiss on his forehead.

'Oh!' said Bertilak. (Gawain was heartily relieved when he did not ask why.)

Next day, Sir Bertilak went hunting again. Gawain stayed in bed and tried to write a song – his last song – to take his mind off the coming New Year's day.

The song was never finished. In came Fidelia, more eager than ever to be with Gawain. He tried to tell her it would be wrong for him to steal kisses which rightfully belonged to her husband. But she only said she loved him all the more for being such a perfect gentleman. In the end, he could not stop her planting a kiss on his left cheek and a kiss on his right.

When Sir Bertilak came home, he had killed a boar in the hunt, and he gave the shining tusks to Gawain. Gawain in answer, gripped him by the elbows and kissed him on both cheeks.

'Well!' said Bertilak, but, to Gawain's relief, did not ask why.

Next day – the last day of the year – Sir Bertilak went hunting once more. Gawain stayed in bed and tried to pray – his last prayers – for next day he must keep his rendezvous with the Green Knight.

His prayers were interrupted, of course. Fidelia bounced on to the bed and demanded to kiss Gawain. Now Fidelia was a very beautiful woman, and Gawain was tempted. After all, by the next day he might be too dead ever to enjoy himself again. Even so, he only allowed Fidelia to kiss him three times, because he did very much want to go to Heaven when he died.

Then Fidelia gave him a present. She unfastened from round her waist a plain green sash. 'Keep this, as a token of my love,' she said.

'No, I mustn't.'

'You think it's too plain to bother with.'

'No, of course not, but I—'

'It isn't. It has magical powers, this belt. The man who wears it can never be killed.'

Now *there* was a temptation Gawain could not resist. He took the sash and wore it over one shoulder, and when Sir Bertilak came home that night, he did not give it up – not even in exchange for the lovely stag Bertilak had taken in the hunt. He did give the kisses.

One.

'Oh!'

Two.

'Well!'

Three.

'Forsooth!'

But Gawain kept the green sash, just in case it was truly magic and could preserve his life.

Next day, Gawain said goodbye to Sir Bertilak and his wife, and rode to keep his appointment, the giant's own axe swinging from his saddle, to and fro, to and fro. A servant from the castle showed him the way – to a green, mossy gorge with a kind of hillock in the centre and a stone doorway in the end of the mound. 'I wouldn't be you for all the gold in Albion,' said the servant and galloped away as fast as his horse would carry him.

'I've come, sir, to keep my promise!' Gawain's voice echoed along the gorge, thin and reedy. He was horribly afraid.

Suddenly the Green Knight stood before him, his head restored to its proper place, his green eyes shining, his green teeth bared in the broadest of smiles. 'Then you have not shamed the knights of Camelot, and you are braver than most men I ever met. Bend your neck, lad, and let me strike my blow, as we agreed one year ago.'

Gawain said a last prayer, knelt down and bent his head. His golden curls flopped forward across his cheeks. The Green Knight retrieved his axe from Gawain's saddle, and raised it high. The noise of its blade slicing the air made Gawain look up. Seeing the cleaver was too much. He dived to one side, sprawling in the mud, and the axehead missed him by a hair's breadth.

'Aah! So you are a coward, after all! Did *I* flinch? Did *I* jump out of the way?'

'Did you have as much to lose?' replied Gawain, picking himself up out of the mud. 'When my head is off, it can't be put back as easily as yours.' But Gawain was ashamed of his cowardice. 'Strike again, sir, and this time I will not flinch,' he said. Clasping his hands to his chest, he bowed his head meekly and closed his eyes.

Up went the axe. The Green Giant grunted with the

strain of swinging it. Down came the axe, and the corner of its blade slashed through the green sash which Gawain wore over one shoulder. It nicked the side of his neck, and blood spurted out, as red as hollyberries.

With a whoop of delight, Gawain leapt to his feet. A blow had been struck, the giant had missed – and Gawain was still alive! He was so overjoyed he could not even feel the pain in his neck. He had never been so happy in his whole life.

The Green Knight did not seem too downcast, either. 'Truly, Gawain,' he said, in an oddly familiar voice, 'truly, you are one of the most excellent knights I've ever met. Not perfect, maybe, but good enough to be proud of yourself. You gave me the one kiss, you gave me the two kisses, you even gave me the three. But the green sash you kept to yourself, and that's why I gave you that nick – a wound to remind you of your little, little lie.'

'*Bertilak!?*'

'Yes, indeed. I asked my wife to test your honesty. You *almost* passed the test, indeed you did! And the only reason you kept the sash was in the hope of staying alive: that's forgivable in any youngster. So let's shake hands and part friends. You've acquitted yourself like a true knight today! Keep the belt. Its colour will remind you of me – and of my pretty wife, I dare say.'

But Gawain's happiness had crumbled. He felt small and foolish and ashamed. He had kept back the sash, broken his promise to a friend, and been found out for the coward he was. He was much, much harder on himself than the Green Knight, whose jolly laugh rang down the green gorge behind him, like a Christmas bell.

He did not try to hide the truth from his fellow knights. The moment Gawain got back to Camelot, he told exactly what had happened, sparing himself none of the shame. The Christmas festivities were being dismantled, the hangings folded away, the boughs of yew burned in the grate.

When they had heard his story, the knights laughed almost as loud as the Green Knight. Arthur took a length of green drapery from round his throne, and tore it into thin strips. 'From now on,' he declared, 'we shall all wear green sashes, to match Gawain's. Why should he be marked out as any different from his fellows? None of us is perfect. It's *trying* that matters.'

So no one ever thought the worse of Gawain for his adventure with the Green Knight – except perhaps Gawain. And that saved him from the sin of pride and made him an altogether better person, if not the perfect knight.

The perfect knight was still to come.

Nine

THE KNIGHT
WITH NO NAME

Once, far from Camelot – beyond the sea, in the realm of France – a woman dressed all in green brought bad news to the castle of Benoic.

'King Ban, master of this house is lost,' she said. 'He has fallen in battle and is dead.'

While the whole castle echoed to the sound of crying, and everyone's eyes were covered, the lady in green went to the cradle of the dead king's baby son, wrapped the child in her cloak and ran lightly away, leaving no footprints on the wet grass.

She stole him out of France, away to the forests of Albion, and there she raised him and taught him – even loved him, with a fierce, imprisoning love. She taught him mysteries known only to women. She taught him how to fight better than any living man, coached him in the chivalric arts of poetry and song, and how to carry himself like a gentleman yet dare anything for a good cause.

Only one thing she failed to teach him, and that was his name. 'That you must find out for yourself,' she would say. People called her the Lady of the Woods.

On the feast of Saint John, she came to Camelot, dressed all in green and veiled, leading by the bridle a white horse and its rider, a handsome young man in white armour, with a shield of white and red. 'If you knight this man,' she told King Arthur, 'he will bring great honour to your Company of the Round Table.'

A cold wind blew in behind her, and set all the doors of Camelot banging. The Lady Nimue, skirts still glistening with the magic of Merlin, put her hand to her heart with a gasp. 'And he will bring great grief, too,' she whispered to herself. 'I feel it. This is where the end begins.'

'By all means, I shall knight him!' exclaimed the King. 'What is his name?'

'Both he and you will find that out in time,' answered the lady. Then she turned and retraced her steps towards the woods, leaving no footprints on the wet grass.

Next morning, the castle chapel was crowded with knights and their ladies, with banners and music and prayers. But the white knight could still be seen pacing up and down outside, running his fingers through his mane of tawny hair. As Queen Guinevere came by on her way into church, she asked in a whisper, 'Is something wrong, young man? Do you fear to be a knight?'

'Not at all!' he groaned, 'But I fear the shame of telling the King that I have . . . *forgotten my sword*!'

The Queen wanted to laugh, but turned away so as not to hurt his feelings. 'Arthur, too, forgot a sword once, when he was young.' She hurried on into the church, but was back a moment later, carrying a sword. 'The knights cannot go armed into church, so they leave their weapons in the porch. Borrow this; no one will know.'

The young man gazed at the Queen with his honey-coloured eyes. 'For this kindness, I shall be your knight and champion for ever and a day,' he said. Guinevere's cheeks coloured and she looked down at her feet. Even as she went into church, she could feel his stare still on her back, like the tip of a sharp sword.

'Arise Sir . . . Knight,' said King Arthur, having no other name with which to dub the young man kneeling at his feet. 'Seek out adventure and fame . . . oh, and a name for yourself – or how shall your place be marked at my Round Table?'

On his very first quest, Fate brought Arthur's newest knight to Sorry Castle, a place filled with such evil that the walls groaned and the stones howled. A maiden sat crying close by.

'Don't go in! Don't try to go in!' she pleaded, hanging on his stirrup, and sobbing. 'The castle is under an enchantment! Any knight who tries to enter has to fight the castle's champion. But even if he wins, another champion comes out – and another, and another! It's impossible to fight them all! That's how my sweetheart died. Turn back before you meet the same fate!'

'Ah now this is a challenge fit for a knight of the Company of King Arthur!' declared the knight-with-no-name, and he rode up at once and rattled the portcullis.

First one knight came out to refuse him entry to Sorry Castle – and then another, and then another. But to the maiden's astonishment, this newcomer hardly tired at all as he felled one with a lance, another with a sword, another trampled by his white horse, another knocked from the saddle with a mailed fist. Ten knights came out to challenge him, and ten lay sprawled on the floor when the portcullis of Sorry Castle at last rattled upwards to allow him inside.

But oh! Inside the first gate was a second! And the second was guarded by a dozen more knights, who set on him all at once, not one at a time! Their axes and flails and swords and lances clattered pitilessly against the white and red shield But it seemed that the harder it was struck, the more strength flowed into the white knight's body, and he fought on tirelessly.

As the last defender fell, the inner gate swung open for the first time in years, breaking the webs which generations of spiders had spun. A great cheer of gratitude went up from the people of Sorry Castle – clearly they were not responsible for the monstrous customs of the castle. A smell of fetid magic and rotting spells made the white knight wrinkle his nose in disgust. Now and then there flitted past his head black bat-like shapes, whistling and keening.

The people clamoured around the hero's horse, clapping his leg-armour, kissing his boots. But their pinched faces were still full of fear.

'Where is the lord of this dreadful place?' he asked.

'Run away!' they answered.

'Quit the castle!'

'Left his enchantments behind!'

'None of us can leave this place alive, unless the Chest of Enchantments is unlocked!'

'Show me,' said the knight wearily. 'I shall try what I can and do what I may.'

The cellars of Sorry Castle were slimy and dark, and shook with noise – howls and groans and screams. The very floor under his feet trembled, and his flesh crawled. Webs broke across his face, snails crunched under his bootsoles, and there was a sound of trickling water, as though the castle itself was weeping.

At the end of a narrow tunnel loomed a door. At first he thought that two copper suits of empty armour stood on either side for decoration, copper axes raised. But in the nick of time, he saw eyes glimmer above the copper visors. Throwing his shield over his back, he fended off the falling axes.

Pushing on through the doorway, he all but hurtled headlong into a gaping hole beyond. Grabbing the brick rim of an open well, he dislodged pebbles which fell away into impenetrable darkness. The splash came from unimaginably far below. Only by clawing for handholds did he keep from plunging down there too.

The smell that rose out of the well was of something rotten and poisonous. Edging his hands and chin around the rim of the well, his body and feet dangling over the abyss, he painfully reached the far side. He reached out for a firm grip – something to pull himself out by . . . and his fingers closed over the metal studded shoe of a foot. He looked up into the face of the Black Guardian!

Black headed, with eyes like burning coals and a mouthful of blue fire, it stamped on the knight's fingers and kicked at his face, trying to dislodge him into the gaping well.

He grabbed hold of one of the bony black ankles and held on. The Guardian staggered; the knight rolled out on to the cell floor and bit deep into the other ankle: it tasted of sulphur and tar. The Guardian, losing its balance, tried to steady itself but toppled backwards into the well. The flame from its screaming mouth lit up the well all the way from top to bottom. Then with a splash the blue flames went out, and the only light left came from a single, tarry torch guttering in a wall-bracket.

The copper statue of a woman stood beside a huge trunk, and from her fingers dangled the keys. The chest itself bristled with copper pipes – as many as the spines on a hedgehog – and out of the pipes came a deafening cacophony of misery: the sounds of Sorry Castle. The knight-with-no-name said a prayer, made the sign of the Cross, then plucked the keys from the statue and fitted them to the locks.

What if the chest were full of demons and curses, spirits from Hell, ghouls or goblins or gremlins? *Clack-clack*, the locks' intricate mechanisms were sprung. The copper pipes coughed out a sulphurous soot, and the noise fell silent.

All over Sorry Castle birds began to sing. Flowers bloomed on the graves of the dead knights, and the two gates fell off their hinges with a shivering crash. Down in the cellars, the copper statue of the maiden

fell sprawling at his feet. It made his heart turn over to see that graven face smile up at him, empty of life ... And it made his heart miss a beat to read, on the underside of the chest's open lid, the words: *WHO RAISES THIS LID IS LANCELOT DU LAC, SON OF KING BAN OF BENOIC, AND THE MOST VALIANT KNIGHT IN THE WORLD.*

Lancelot du Lac rode back to Camelot to inform King Arthur of his true name. But the King already knew. For invisible powers had burned the words into the backrest of his rightful seat at the Round Table. Guinevere saw them first. And many times, during the next few days, she could be seen brushing her fingers over the magical letters: *Lancelot du Lac.*

His was not the Seat of Mortal Danger, but stood close to it. Very close indeed.

Ten

A TRICK
OF THE HEART

*H*e fought bandits and brigands, monsters and tyrants, invaders, interlopers and assassins. He rescued women and children, villages and strongholds – even knights of the Round Table who met with enemies more powerful than they. On a field of battle, no one, it seemed, was more powerful than Sir Lancelot du Lac – not even King Arthur. On the tournament field, he won every prize – even the great diamond that was offered each year at the Christmas joust. Year by year, diamond by diamond, the fame grew of Arthur's 'best of all knights'.

'Isn't he the finest man a realm could hope for?' Arthur said to Guinevere, bursting with pride. 'Isn't God to be thanked for sending him to Camelot?'

But Guinevere only bent her head lower over her

needlework, her cheeks burning and her mouth dry. Her heart thudded so loudly that she thought the room must ring with the sound of it.

'And *you* should thank God for sending you such a champion!' exclaimed Arthur, hearing nothing.

'Oh I do, my lord, I do,' said Guinevere. 'Every day of my life.'

Riding on his latest quest, Sir Lancelot looked up at Guinevere's scarf fluttering at the tip of his lance: her favour, her gift. And he felt a pang of joy. He found himself at the very centre of the Waste Land, and against the skyline, blotting out the setting sun, rose the ruined Castle Corbenic, home of King Pelles. Lancelot decided to rest there for the night, if the good king was willing to entertain him. But as he rode towards it, he had the strangest feeling that he was being watched.

'Here he comes,' said the woman in black to King Pelles. 'So. You wish him to marry your daughter, Fair Elayne. That he will never do by choice.'

'He must, or the prophecy cannot come true, and nothing can come to any good!' The old king lay in his bed by the window, his face re-carved by pain, the bedclothes thrown back from the terrible wound in his thigh. Ever since Balin had struck that terrible, mistaken blow, and the castle had crumbled, and the countryside

withered, King Pelles' wound had refused to heal. He neither died nor recovered, just like the landscape outside his window.

'His heart is set on one woman and one woman only,' said the woman in black. 'Lancelot loves Queen Guinevere. His heart is sealed up against any other woman, like a thing walled up in a tower.'

The king stirred angrily amid his pillows. 'Is this why you came calling on me? To tell me what I already know? I thought you said you could help me!'

'I can,' said the woman. Her face was hidden by a hood, her fingers by the cuffs of her black dress. 'I can make the prophecy come true. Elayne and Lancelot will be mother and father to a boy . . . if you trust to my *special* arts.'

Pelles imagined her ugly inside that hood, a hideous crone seared dry by the steam of a witch's cauldron. But her voice was soothing and musical. He said, 'Try what you can and do what you may. Unless the prophecy comes true, I shall never be healed, and the Waste Land will spread out to the last ledges of the world.'

So Lancelot was made welcome at Castle Corbenic. The place was in ruins, but though starlight glimmered through the gaping walls, and owls roosted among the broken roof timbers, the banquet set before him was as fine as any given at Camelot. The King's pretty daughter, Lady Elayne, sat shyly opposite – a charming, sweet-natured girl who gasped with wonder as Lancelot recounted his battle that day with a dragon.

'Did you never think to marry?' asked King Pelles casually. He reclined on a couch, his leg cushioned on sheepskins. 'A fighting man needs the comfort and prayers of a wife.'

'My heart is given to a lady already, I'm afraid,' Lancelot admitted, smiling brightly at Elayne. 'I can never love anyone but her.' And Elayne drooped like a cut flower.

Someone replenished the visitor's wine; he did not see who. It tasted richer, redder, spicier afterwards, and it fuddled his brains. He did not remember going to bed – only the stars teeming like snow beyond the gaping ceiling of his chamber. There was no candle or lamp in the room.

When someone entered, Lancelot raised himself on one elbow: 'Who's there?'

'It is I, my love. Guinevere. Your lady love.'

'Guinevere?! But the King! . . .?'

'Hush. Arthur is king of my life and of my land. But only you will ever be master of my love.'

'How did you get here? How did you know . . .?'

'Your adventures blaze a trail bright as any comet. Now hush and hold me.'

The stars, the wine, the magic in the wine all did their work. Lancelot folded her in his arms and rained as many kisses on her as the stars overhead were raining on the Earth.

At daybreak, Lancelot woke. The room gradually filled up with honey-coloured light, like the nectar cupped in a flower. He turned to rejoice in Guinevere's face, and saw beside him . . . the Fair Elayne.

'What are you doing here? What do you want with me?'

'Your love,' she whispered, shrinking away.

'Never!'

'Didn't my kisses taste sweet last night – as sweet as hers?'

'I was bewitched!'

'Yes, I admit it. But it was your Fate. My Fate. To have your child. To have your son.'

Lancelot scrabbled together the pieces of clothing and armour strewn around the room. He was panic-stricken, horrified at what he had done. He fumbled with his boots, cut himself on his spurs. Drops of blood fell on to the sheets. He fled Castle Corbenic, and galloped back to Camelot.

But the news had travelled even faster. Guinevere already knew. How? She knew already how he had taken the Lady Elayne as a lover and given her his kisses.

She turned on him a look like the lidless basilisk whose eyes can turn a man to stone. 'I hear she is very *beautiful*,' said Guinevere, as cold as ice. Lancelot fled those eyes, and hid himself among the brambles beside Camelot's nettly moat.

Morgan le Fay laughed long and loud as she sealed up her flagon of magic wine. She congratulated herself on sowing the seeds of shame at Arthur's court. Shame. It would grow now, mossy and envious green, up the walls of Camelot.

Shame.

Poor Elayne. Once her baby had been born, she was left with nothing but shame. Lancelot, the love of her life, had left her. The child was placed in safe keeping at a monastery: Elayne kissed him, blessed him with a name, then let go her hold on him. She let go, too, her hold on life. Her father's kingdom was a Waste Land where spring never came. But Elayne's heart was a greater Waste Land still.

'When I am dead,' she told her father, 'lay me in a boat, and set the boat

on the river.' She wrote a note. It read: '*Here lies the Fair Elayne, who loved, but was never loved.*'

Like a million tears, the river carried dead Elayne away from the Castle Corbenic, across the Waste Land, and along a meandering course to Camelot.

One day, as muddy Lancelot crouched beside the moat, the wind rippled the water and broke the surface into strings of diamond sunlight. Suddenly he recalled his tourney treasure – the diamonds won year by year at the Christmas joust. Perhaps *that* was the gift to win Guinevere's forgiveness.

He ran to fetch them, scrubbed his face, changed his clothes and presented himself before the Queen. What did it matter that the room was crowded? What did it matter what people thought?

'Lady! I your champion have disappointed you. Let me therefore surrender to you the prizes I won when I carried your favour on the point of my lance – my tourney treasure!'

Every woman in the room stared and gasped with wonder. Every woman but Guinevere, that is.

'This is mine?' she said, holding up the necklace of priceless diamonds. 'Mine to do with as I choose?'

'Of course. As is my life!' declared Lancelot, on bended knees.

Guinevere tipped back her face and sniffed with

scorn. Then she went to the window and tossed the gems far out into the river below. As they fell, they split the sunlight into a dozen rainbows.

The whole court stampeded towards the window. They leaned out, pointing and shrieking, trying to see where the necklace had fallen.

The diamonds had sunk from sight. But the knights and courtiers caught sight of something else on the river – at first indistinct, then more clearly a boat, then more clearly still a cargo of flowers and white samite.

Down at the river bank, King Arthur tugged at the sad little note, and its corner tore off in the dead girl's stiff fingers. He read it to himself: '*Here lies the Fair Elayne, who loved, but was never loved.*' Wiping away a tear, he gave orders for Elayne to be buried with all ceremony and gentleness. When he showed the note to his wife, however, he was surprised to see that it brought a flicker of pure joy to her face.

'*. . . but was never loved.*' She mouthed the words silently.

Guinevere chose not to sleep in the King's bed that night. She said she was unwell, and would sleep in another room. And though there were bars at the window and guards near the door, such strength was in Lancelot's arms that he bent the iron bars at the window of Guinevere's bedchamber, and climbed inside.

Guinevere and Lancelot were in love – not as champion and lady any longer, but as man and woman. That was plain to see, for anyone with eyes. The wonder was that Arthur stayed blind to their love.

Eleven

TWO SONS

Time rolled on like the wheel of a cart, crushing the days, crushing the years. The river rolled by Camelot, stranding on its banks ears of corn, empty birds' eggs, chains of daisies. One day it was a boat with a girl's body in it, another a slab of red marble, floating. There was a sword buried up to the hilt in its veiny heart. Years had come and gone betweenwhiles, but the river had no grasp of Time. One day it left a boat, another a stone, and in it wedged a sword.

'This is Merlin's work,' said Arthur.

'What does it mean? What does the writing say?' everyone asked, lining the river bank, leaning gingerly out over the water. Sir Gawain read out the inscription still shining in gold letters around the red slab: '*NONE SHALL DRAW THIS SWORD BUT THE PUREST KNIGHT IN THE WORLD* . . . That's not me,' said Gawain, fingering the green sash across his chest.

'Nor me' said Bedevere.

'Nor me,' said Agravain.

They looked towards Lancelot, hero of so many adventures.

'No!' said Lancelot sharply. 'No.' Suddenly his conscience weighed in his chest heavy as red marble. 'It must mean the King.'

All eyes turned on Arthur. But even he would not lay claim to the title on the rock. Besides, he had a sword already.

Mystified, they turned back to the castle. Perhaps the stone was destined to float on down the river.

During dinner, visitors were announced. A nun entered ahead of a young knight in scarlet armour. His hair was a coppery red, and his skin very fair with freckles which made him look even younger than his years – a child almost. The Court had never seen him before. Or had they? He was so much like someone they knew ... The knights racked their brains to think whom.

For Lancelot, it was like looking in a mirror.

'This is Galahad,' said the nun, 'son of Lancelot du Lac and Elayne of Corbenic. The time has come for him to take his place at the Round Table.'

Lancelot stared at Galahad, living proof of his awful sin – and yet the finest thing he had ever achieved: a boy, a son, a knight. There was something so excellent about the young man in red, that no one could think less of him for his unfortunate beginnings. The ladies noticed the colour of his eyes. The men noticed that he had no weapon. What they also noticed, as Galahad strode round the Table, was that he meant to sit down in the only empty seat – the Seat of Mortal Danger.

'*No! Not there!*' cried Lancelot. Separated from his son by the breadth of the Table, he leapt on to it, sliding across the planed surface on hands and knees. But he was too late. He covered his face with his hands. Was this his punishment, then? To meet his son in one moment and see him burned to death the next? Not bearable!

But Galahad lowered himself into the Seat of Mortal Danger, where no man had ever sat. And no column of fire engulfed him. No ravens swooped on his head. When the other knights crowded round him, they could already read his name in raised gold letters, across the back of the seat: SIR GALAHAD.

'Ah. I'm afraid not, Chair,' said Galahad, reading it over his shoulder. 'Not "Sir". How can I be a knight without a sword?'

'Come with me!' exclaimed Arthur, and dragging Galahad by the wrist, hurried him down the terraces of Camelot to the river's edge. The red marble slab still lay, half sunk in ooze, a dove perched on its swordhilt. '*There* is your sword,' said the King.

Galahad took two strides into the water and pulled out

the sword as easily as a needle from red cloth. He seemed a little taken aback by the noisy cheering which greeted this simple task. 'Life at Camelot,' he thought to himself, 'seems very merry.'

That night, after a church service and the knighting of Galahad, Lancelot sat and watched his son across the debris of a feast. He had been a young man when Elayne had tricked her way into his bed. He remembered as if it had happened yesterday. And yet the boy was now a grown man. That made Lancelot old. He examined his reflection in his spoon – the greying hair, the scars . . . Then Guinevere glanced up and smiled, and that made him young again.

Suddenly, with a gust of wind which extinguished all the candles, the great doors blew open and someone entered. No, there was no one there. Only a square of white silk. It floated into the room and circled the hall, filling it with the sweetest perfume that ever blew off a field of flowers. Under the silk was something solid, round – a bowl? a dish? – and in that bowl a light brighter than crumbled stars or the embers of a sun. The room was bright and brighter than day. The straw-strewn floor smoked with light. The birds roosting in the rafters broke into a dawn chorus.

Not a man or woman could speak, blink or turn their face away, so that the mysterious vessel burned itself into their memories. No gold letters blazoned it, no herald announced it, no druid intoned the magic of its coming. And yet they all knew what they were seeing. Here was the Holy Grail – the chalice into which the blood of Jesus Christ ran down, as He died upon the Cross. What magic might be released, if only that cloth were removed! Christ's blood had been washing away Man's sins for so many centuries. What miracles might this cup perform if only a man could lay hands on it!

The Holy Grail, under its veil of silk, hovered for a time above the Round Table – then vanished, the square of samite fluttering down and melting into the wood like hawfrost. Each witness was free to lower his eyes – and found the plate in front of him filled with his favourite food.

'Oysters!' said Gawain, first to regain his voice.

'Venison!' said the King.

'Lion's meat!' said Lancelot.

In front of Galahad lay freshly baked bread, as plain as plain.

'We were not fit to see it,' said the King, as delight gave way to sorrow. 'If only we could have seen it uncovered!'

'That vision was sent to us for a reason,' said Sir Bedevere.

'It was a summons,' said Sir Lancelot.

'To a quest!' cried Sir Gawain.

The coming of the Grail had put from their minds completely the new member of their Company. Now

Galahad got up and said, 'God willing, I mean to see that cup of bliss unveiled before I die. With your blessing, my lord, I shall leave tomorrow.'

'And I!'

'And I!'

'And I!' cried the Company of the Round Table.

'Do it!' said King Arthur rising to his feet. 'Light your torches at Camelot's hearth, water your horses at Camelot's well, then go with my blessing. God alone knows what miracles you may see!'

In her house, a two-hour ride away, Morgan le Fay also sat down to dine. No Grail appeared to her, but there was a visitor, a Knight of the Company of the Round Table. He was far younger than she, with long black hair and a black moustache which dripped to either side of his mouth like candle wax.

'Good evening, my dear, my darling,' he said.

'Good evening, my beau, my bird. What news?'

He recounted the day's events at Camelot. She was horrified, but he soothed her: 'They'll never find their "Holy Grail". It takes saints to see such things, and there's not one saint among the lot of them.'

Morgan was less sure. 'What about this new knight, Galahad? Lancelot's boy. You say he sat in the Seat of Mortal Danger? That makes him the purest knight in the world.'

'Then he's too good to live, and God will take him for an angel,' sneered her lover. 'As for the rest! There's Gawain with his green sash . . .'

'Bedevere who tells lies . . .'

'Chivalrous Bors who prefers ladies to religion . . .'

'Nimue with Merlin on her conscience . . .'

'Lancelot and Guinevere with so very *much* to be sorry for . . .' They laughed together at that.

'And Arthur,' said he.

'And Arthur,' said she. 'I've told you how Arthur wronged me. Tell me again why *you* hate him.'

Mordred half closed his black eyes and began to plait the side strands of his hair. 'Once upon a time,' he said, smiling, 'Arthur whispered love to my mother. But he left her with nothing but tears to weep and a baby in her arms. Yes, just as Lancelot did with Elayne. Noble, courteous Arthur. Goody-good Arthur. He's as flawed as all the rest. But now that baby is grown. Now the King of Albion has a grown son among his knights! – even if he doesn't know it yet. Now they have Prince Mordred to reckon with!'

'So let's knit together our hate for him, my sweeting,' said Morgan gloatingly, 'as the sea gathers its waves to drown the land.'

Mordred covered her hand with his. 'They think this a glorious night – the beginning of the Grail Quest – the start of some Golden Age. But I'll tell you something, my joy, my jewel: that Company of happy knights will never sit down together again in friendship. The seams of the Round Table are cracking tonight.'

'Are they, Mordred? Are they?'

'Oh yes. After all, the wood that made it grew in *our* domain, didn't it? In the dark and magic forest. Not out there, in the sunlight.'

Twelve

GRAIL QUEST

Some went one way, some went another, alone or in pairs. Tempted by demons, watched by angels, up and down the length of Albion the Knights of King Arthur went questing after the Holy Grail. Farther and farther afield they looked, across the Waste Land, across the Borders, across the sea, across the world.

But some strayed from the Quest to rescue maidens, others to joust. Some deposed tyrants and others captured kingdoms and stayed to be kings. Some met faeries, and some met fiends. Some found treasure, and stayed to spend it. Some languished in dungeons and some dined in palaces. Some lived and some died.

King Arthur made a great book, from leather and parchment, and his scribe wrote down the adventures of those who returned from their Grail Quest.

Three knights ended their search on the sea-shore, though on different beaches: Sir Bors, Sir Perceval and

Sir Galahad. Each found himself at the foot of a gangplank, beckoned aboard ship.

The ships were clinkered with magic, had sails of white silk and no crew to haul them. The course they steered was stranger still, for they carried Sir Bors, Sir Perceval and Sir Galahad overland. And when the ships hove to, in mid-air, their anchors grappled the towers and turrets of Corbenic Castle as they might some undersea reef. Bors, Perceval and Galahad awoke, reunited, in the ruined castle of King Pelles. The King seemed to be expecting them.

His pain now was terrible to see. The wound in his leg had bled for twenty years. The rain had rained in through his rafters, the moorland animals had blundered through his rooms. His outlook on every side, was of blasted trees, sickly yellow grass and putrid lakes. And his daughter was dead. Yet his courtesy never wavered.

'Sit down and welcome, sirs,' he told the Round Table knights. One clap of his hands broke the frost on the sills; doves in the rafters shook loose a snowfall of white feathers.

At the same moment, outside, in the orchard, Sir Lancelot du Lac dismounted from his horse to walk the last few paces. If he had realized where he was, he would never have called at Castle Corbenic. Too many bad memories. But Lancelot was lost, and the night was very dark, with castling rainclouds blotting out the moon. He approached the place unwittingly, thinking to ask where he was and for shelter from the coming storm.

But the path through the orchard seemed uncommonly winding and steep. The leafless apple trees pointed bony twigs at him and the wind blew so hard in his face that he could barely take one step forward. Wrapping his cloak tightly round him, Lancelot sank down to the ground and was asleep before his cheek touched the earth. Asleep, but dreaming.

The storm broke just as a maiden entered King Pelles' hall. Jagged blades of lightning pierced the castle walls, but she did not flinch. She carried a silver table and on it something veiled in white silk.

'The Holy Grail!' breathed Bors.

'Our quest ends here,' said Perceval.

'All these years I've waited,' said the bedridden King. 'All these years I've prayed. All these years I've suffered so that you might understand. Here is the end of every journey.'

'It was here all along!' said Bors under his breath. 'Pelles is the Guardian of the Grail as well as the Spear!'

'One of our Company of Knights wounded him,' Perceval began.

'Now one of us must heal him!' Bors concluded.

The maiden carrying the silver table set it down and

looked into the face of Sir Bors. He saw she had long red hair.

The maiden moved on to Sir Perceval. He saw she had long red hair and a face as bright as snow.

The maiden stood face to face with Galahad. He saw that she had long red hair, a face as bright as snow, and towering wings of golden feathers couched behind her back. He walked to the silver table and drew the silk from the chalice. Then he carried the Holy Grail to the bed where King Pelles lay. Then he let some of the liquid inside pour on to the wound, and put the Grail to the King's lips.

Instantly a youthfulness returned to King Pelles which twenty years of suffering had stolen away. He stood up and danced and laughed and shouted: 'Thank God! Thank God! I've waited so long for you to come, bold Sir Galahad!' The words rebounded from the arches of a perfect vaulted ceiling. The walls of Corbenic healed and knit together, leaving no scar. The trees in the orchard put on leaves and apples, and the grass beneath the sleeping knight grew green. Over four counties trees flexed, all green again with sap. Rivers laughed over waterfalls, the corn sprouted, almost ready for reaping.

Galahad said to the angel, 'I have seen what I was born to see, and what I lived to see. Now if God will let me, I should like to leave this world and be with Him.'

As he held the Holy Grail, a flock of laughing angels

mobbed the young knight and carried him swiftly away. Their spread wings enfolded him. Bors and Perceval were left kneeling in prayer, while Pelles danced between them and around them, singing for sheer joy.

All this Lancelot saw – not clearly, but through a smear of sleep. It was like peering through the smoke of a forest fire. He tried to get up, to get closer, to reach the Holy Grail. But he could not move. He tried to call out to the Grail maiden, but his voice stuck in his throat like a stone.

As the broken walls healed and Castle Corbenic became whole again, Lancelot was plunged into darkness. The trees blossomed round him. The rain began. Down the orchard path came an old man and his page, each carrying a candle, though the wind and rain did not stir the candle flames. As they passed Lancelot, the page peered down.

'You would have thought this fellow would want to see the Grail.'

'I expect he was too weighed down with sin,' said the old man.

Then they were gone. So, too, were the chains which had seemed to bind

Lancelot to the ground. He could move once more. 'Now, by my son's hand, I swear I'll never sin again!' he called, but there was no one to hear his vow. 'Never! Never! Never!' He groped his way to his feet and out of the orchard, the torrential rain streaming down his face no faster than his tears.

Back at Camelot, Bors and Perceval recounted to King Arthur the last chapter of his leather book. They told how Galahad alone had held the Holy Grail and joined the angels at God's Round Table.

'And you, Lancelot,' said Arthur. 'Were you there when your son achieved his greatest victory?'

'No,' said Lancelot. 'No. I couldn't . . . I wasn't . . . I was too . . .'

The scribe bending over the open book blinked his rheumy eyes. The ink dried on his quill nib, waiting.

'I was too sinful,' said Lancelot. A murmur ran round the room.

'Surely not! Surely!' said Arthur smiling. 'What sin weighs so heavy on your conscience?' Lancelot did not answer, but whispers murmured like a sea tide rising.

'I know what sin!' called Sir Agravain.

'Keep quiet,' said Gawain. But Agravain would not.

'I know what sin *he* has on his conscience! And it's time the King knew it, too!'

Thirteen

BURNING

*G*awain bundled his brother out into the yard and shook him. 'Who put you up to this? You're not a spiteful man! Why would you want to destroy Lancelot?'

'Sir Mordred and I have been talking,' said Agravain. 'We agree. A Christian company of knights should not tolerate such sins.'

'Ah! Sir Mordred, was it? I never trusted that man.' Gawain looked into Agravain's face. 'What do you hope to achieve? Break the King's heart? Disband the Company of the Round Table? For what?'

But priggish Agravain shook off his brother. 'Say what you like, I'm going to tell. Your own sons agree with me. Florence and Lovel. They'll do it if I don't.'

'Tell me what?' said the King, following them out into the yard.

'It's nothing,' said Gawain.

'My honour demands that I speak!' declared Agravain pompously. 'The truth is, my lord . . .'

'Hold your tongue!' begged Gawain.

'The truth is, the Queen your wife and Lancelot du Lac are lovers and have been this many a year!'

All colour drained from Arthur's face. The sun went behind a cloud. He did not speak until it came out again.

'I don't believe it. Not a word. I trust my wife past all suspicion. Let me hear no more of these lies.' He turned on his heel to go back indoors. His hand was on the doorhanging when Sir Mordred's voice rang out across the yard.

'What if you had proof, my lord? What then?'

Next day, King Arthur announced that he was going hunting, and rode out of Camelot with half his court: a cavalcade of coloured doublets, trailing horsecloths and a babble of hounds.

Guinevere sent for Lancelot.

All of his good resolve, all of the promises he had made to God and to himself were forgotten.

'Don't go,' urged Sir Bors. 'I have a fear in me like a nagging tooth.'

'But the Queen has sent for me,' said Lancelot lightly. 'I am her champion, you know. How can I not go when she summons me?'

'At least put on some armour!' said Bors. 'I have a fear in me like a stone in my boot.' But Lancelot had already gone.

He went directly to the Queen's room, and when he saw her eyes and smelled the perfume of her, there seemed nothing to do but kiss. Galahad had found his heart's desire in the Holy Grail. Lancelot found it only in Guinevere.

'*Come out, Lancelot du Lacklustre!*' came a shout through the door. '*Surrender yourself!*'

'*And pay for your lechery!*'

'*And die for your treachery!*'

Guinevere squealed into the hollow of Lancelot's throat. Lancelot rolled off the bed and pulled on his shirt. There was no window to the room, no other way out. '*Mordred!*' he hissed.

'Oh God, we're betrayed! Now we'll both die!' sobbed Guinevere. Fists were beating on the door now, a great many fists.

'Is there any armour in this room? I can't fight without armour.'

'There is none. Anyway, listen to them; there must be fifteen men out there!'

Lancelot picked up his sword and wrapped his cloak round his other arm. He kissed Guinevere tenderly. 'Pray for me if I die, lady.'

'If you die, do you think I shall go on living?'

Lancelot shouted through the door: 'Please! Don't make me fight you! A man shouldn't fight his comrades! If I have to fight, some of us will be killed.'

But the beating on the door only grew louder. '*Then give yourself up, Lancelot du Lackcourage! Give yourself up and die!*'

Lancelot said a prayer, asking forgiveness for the blood he was about to shed. Then he threw open the door, and a clutter of silver blades thrust into the room, more than the twigs in a witch's broom. Lancelot sheltered behind the door till the swordhands came into view, then he slashed down on them with his sword and hurled himself on his ambushers.

Every man was there who had ever envied Lancelot his skill, his fame or his lover: Mordred had made sure of that. But fourteen strong knights were no match for the best warrior in the world, cornered and desperate. Lancelot killed men he loved, that afternoon, men he had shared wine with, prayed with, eaten with, fought alongside. He killed Sir Agravain, Sir Florence, Sir Lovel, knowing, as he drove home his blade, the grief he was giving Gawain. He killed ten more besides, but Mordred – ah Mordred the mischief-maker – was only cut across the face and fingers, and across the black plait down his back, as he turned to run.

Lancelot fought his way to the gate, he fought his way out on to the greensward. But though he got clear away, his milk-white horse was sprinkled with blood and the cloak round his arm was cut to green ribbons. Nor was the Queen cradled in the crook of his arm. He had left her behind in Camelot. And that was now the most dangerous place in the world for her to be.

'I don't believe it! No, not a word,' said the King, standing amid the corpses of his knights. 'No, no, no.'

'You could ask him . . . if he hadn't run away,' said Mordred licking the blood from his fingers, like jam. Arthur did not seem to hear.

'My lord, don't believe these lies!' Gawain burst in. 'I'm sure some innocent errand brought Lancelot here. I'm sure he never . . .'

'Gawain, the man just killed your brother and your two sons,' said the King, bewildered. 'And you still defend him?'

'They brought their deaths on themselves,' said Gawain, white faced. 'I warned them not to do this. I won't blame Lancelot for defending himself against them. The Queen, my lord . . .'

'Ah yes, the Queen.' Arthur spoke in a high, tuneless voice, wistful and dazed and undone. 'Merlin tried to warn me, you know? And the law must be upheld.'

Mordred licked the blood from the rim of his open mouth, like a cat well-fed.

Arthur said, in the tones of a man asleep, 'Build a fire in the courtyard and let the Queen be burned for a traitor and a whore. When I lay hands on Lancelot, I shall kill him myself.' Gawain begged Arthur to delay the execution – to give time for all sides of the story to be told. He knew that if he could just make the King pause and reflect, Arthur would think better of killing his beloved wife. Above all, the Round Table *must* hold, or the Kingdom of Albion would splinter like ice on the face of a lake.

'You are a good man and a loyal knight,' said Arthur to Gawain. 'There is a service you can do for me.'

'Anything, my liege.'

'You can put on your best armour and escort Gui – the Queen to the stake, for burning.'

'No, sir. That I cannot do. It would go against my conscience and the duty I owe to my rightful Queen and to a dear, good lady. I will not do you that service.'

'*Then have your brothers do it!*' snapped Arthur nastily. '*The only two Lancelot has left alive, I mean.*'

With a roll of drums, Queen Guinevere was led out of the keep doorway. Dressed only in her shift, her hair unfastened and her feet bare, she began the long walk to the bonfire. A heap of green furze had been piled at the base of a wooden stake, and round the stake – like the serpent around the tree in Eden – snaked a silver chain.

At either side of Guinevere, Gawain's brothers, Gareth and Gaheris, walked like men themselves condemned. Though they carried pikes, they wore no armour, for they preferred to call themselves Guinevere's companions rather than her guard. Only a direct order from the King had forced them to perform this terrible duty. Arthur was not there at all – would not, could not bring himself to watch her die.

At every window a woman's face wept – a hundred fluttering white handkerchiefs at a hundred windows. To either side of the stake, a priest stood with a blazing torch. The drumskins split, too brittle in the morning frost.

At the sudden silence, Lancelot du Lac, outside the castle, pulled up his horse's head and plunged in his spurs. 'Now God and my friends help me!' he cried. 'For Love's sake, let us save the Queen!'

Sir Bors, Ector, Lavane, Urry, Lionel and a dozen knights beside, spurred their horses in his wake. In under the portcullis they thundered, their horses' hooves louder than any drumbeat. Just as the silver chain was wound round Guinevere's body, a whirlwind of warriors whooped into the yard, their flying blades a blur of light.

The priests by the bonfire flung their torches in to the furze and fled. There was chaos and shouting. Sudden thick, black smoke added to the confusion. Gaheris threw up his pike in delight to think the Queen would be rescued after all . . . Lancelot mistook it for a lunge, and killed him where he stood. Then Gareth, seeing his brother fall, ran blindly at Lancelot, and died on the point of his spear. With a bloodstained fist, Lancelot pulled Guinevere from the fire, her hems already alight. The silver chain, dragging along the ground behind the milk-white horse, left a trail as far as the edge of the wild wood.

When the news was taken to Arthur that his wife had been rescued and carried away to Lancelot's castle in the north, his heart gave a bound of relief. A sob of pure joy escaped him.

But Gawain took no joy in the Queen's rescue. For both his brothers – all his brothers – were dead at the hand of Lancelot du Lac. He put his hand to his heart – the heart which had harboured such love for the knight-in-white. 'They had no armour. They had no quarrel with him. They had no cause to die,' he said, and then he swore an oath:

BURNING

'Between Sir Lancelot du Lac and I,
let there be no peace, no truce, no rest,
until one of us lies dead,
I by his hands, or he by mine.'

Fourteen

REVENGE

When Gawain loved Lancelot as a friend, there was no friend to match him. But when Gawain's love turned to hatred, there was no hate its equal. He buckled on his armour, belted on his sword and presented himself to the King.

'Well? Is war declared? War against Lancelot du Lac?'

'War, yes,' said the King. 'And death to Sir Lancelot!' But then the tears brimmed over his lids, his shoulders slumped, and he and Gawain held each other close and wept. 'Oh God! This will be the end of everything! The Round Table may as well be broken up for firewood! Half my knights are with him, the rest are baying for his blood. Oh nephew! That it should come to this!'

An army marched out of Camelot next day and followed in the hoofprints of Lancelot all the way to his castle in the north: Castle Joyful. It seemed ill-named now, for all its white walls and pretty campaniles. Month after month, Arthur besieged it. Each day the portcullis would fly up, and out would come knights to do battle with their former comrades. But Lancelot was never among them.

'Come out and fight me, Lancelot du Lac! I've sworn to kill you or die in the attempt!' yelled Gawain.

'That I will not,' Lancelot called down from the walls. 'I'll fight neither you nor the King. I want nothing but to serve my rightful master and to call Gawain my friend!'

'Then why did you kill my brothers? Why Gareth and Gaheris? They weren't even in armour, you dog, and you cut them down!'

'I never meant . . . I never saw . . .'

'Liar!'

'Even so, I won't fight you, Gawain.'

'Then you're a coward as well as a liar, and I'll carve my way in to you if I have to hack away your walls one grain a day!'

At last Lancelot realized that nothing could prevent a fight between him and Gawain. He blunted his lances and he dulled his blade, and he grimed his shield, because he took no pride in fighting a friend. He rode out under his portcullis, he and his knights, to face the mounted strength of Camelot. 'Remember,' he said over his shoulder, 'let no man injure the King or my friend Gawain.'

At the sight of the man who had taken his wife, Arthur levelled his lance and came full tilt across the castle's lawn. He made directly for Lancelot, but though the knight-in-white raised his shield in self defence, he did not couch his lance. He would die rather than fight his rightful king.

Luckily, Arthur's horse dropped a foot into a rabbit hole and stumbled. Arthur was thrown heavily on to his back, and lay stunned for a moment, seeing only part of the sky through a twisted visor.

But no axe fell on his face, no mace hammered on his armour, no horse trampled him into the turf. Only a single hand offered to help him to his feet. Lancelot had dismounted to go to the aid of his king.

'Please,' he said, helping Arthur on to his horse. 'Let's end this war between us, before it does more harm than can ever be put right.'

Arthur laid a hand on his swordhilt, but he did not draw. His eyes were suddenly full of tears as he watched Lancelot remount. 'God knows, you always were the most chivalrous knight in Christendom. Can we not settle this thing like Christians? What are we, dogs squabbling over raw meat?'

They both looked up. Guinevere stood on the battlements of Castle Joyful, her hair blowing like a tattered banner, her face a picture of sadness.

Lancelot shut his eyes, as though in pain. 'A wife

should be with her husband,' he said, 'with a champion to defend her against the world. That is how it was and that is how it should be again.'

'And by God, that's how it *shall* be!' exclaimed Arthur. Their horses moved together and they reached out to shake hands.

'*Defend yourself or die dishonoured!*' yelled a voice hoarse with hatred. Gawain came at Lancelot out of the low sunlight. There was foam in his beard and sweat on his cheek, and a kind of madness in his bloodshot eyes.

Lancelot threw up his shield. The horses cannoned flank against flank, and sparks flew where the knights' grieves clashed. Gawain's sword swung like the sails of a mill. There was no tiring him; his wellspring of hatred gave him the energy to fight on and on, without pause for breath.

Even so, Lancelot was the best knight in the world, and his skill was greater than Gawain's. Like a man savaged by his own dog, Lancelot knew he must strike and strike hard, or die. He landed a blow to Gawain's head which stove in his helmet and split his skull to let in all the stars. Gawain sprawled helpless along the ground.

'Kill me now and make your triumph complete,' he groaned, blinded by his own blood. 'You have killed all my kin, now send me over the borders of Death to be with them!'

'Not I,' said a voice close by. 'Never. Kill my friend? Not if my life depended on it.'

'Oh but it does, it does,' panted Gawain. 'Let me live and I shall come back to fight you. Wound me with ninety-nine wounds and I will come back to fight you a hundredth time!'

The next Gawain knew, he was lying in Arthur's tent, wrapped in blankets and as weak as willow. For weeks he lingered between life and death, tended by the King in person. In his fever he thought he saw the shadow of a lady on horseback move across the canvas wall of the tent. 'It's Morgan le Fay,' he whispered. 'Warn the King!'

133

But it was only Guinevere, riding south to Camelot, leaving her lover behind for ever. Arthur would have ridden with her, but for having his nephew to care for; Gawain could not be moved.

One day, the injured man called for sword, armour and lance.

'And you hardly fit to stand?' said the King soothingly. 'Where do you think you are going?'

'To fight Lancelot du Lac,' Gawain replied.

'But Lancelot and I have ended our quarrel, nephew. For the good of Albion, we've mended the rift between us.'

'Not bricks nor iron nor wood could ever bridge the rift between that man and me. I'll fight him till the sun gutters, till the moon falls down, till the seas dry up. I have sworn it!'

And not even a King can cancel a knight's oath struck with Heaven. So as soon as Gawain could stand, he put on armour, and as soon as he could lift a sword, he mounted up. As soon as he could draw breath he bawled his challenge at the walls of Castle Joyful. '*Come out Lancelot du Lac, and fight! Defend your honour if you have any!*'

Inside the castle, Lancelot let out a heartfelt groan. 'Now God who made the Red Sea part, can you not part us two, and save me from killing my best friend?'

Wearily Lancelot pulled on his armour, unwillingly

mounted his horse, sadly gave orders for the portcullis to be raised. His heart was full, this morning, of the most terrible foreboding.

But when he emerged on to the castle apron, Gawain was nowhere to be seen. The pitched tents of Arthur's army strewed the ground like fallen washing. Carts were being loaded with tent poles and cooking pots. Smiths were shoeing horses . . . Arthur was striking camp, and in a hurry, too.

'What's happened? What's wrong?' he shouted at a page who ran past.

'It's Mordred of the Black Hair! He's seized Camelot! He's made a proclamation! – See?' The boy thrust a rolled parchment into Lancelot's hand, and ran on. Lancelot unrolled it and read:

Let it be known that since the tragic death of our dear King Arthur on campaign in the north, I, Mordred, his natural son, shall reign in his place. Let all Albion bend a loyal knee and cry, "Long life to Mordred, King of Albion and Master of the Round Table." '

Arthur's company of knights circled him round, their horses nodding their heads and ploughing the grass to mud. Both Gawain and Lancelot were there – all those who had sided with the King, all those who had sided with Lancelot. Reunited, they raised their lances, and the sharp tips clattered together against a bright sky.

'*Death to Mordred the Usurper!*' they cried. '*Death and dishonour to the traitor Mordred!*'

'Thank you, my good and loyal companions,' said Arthur, mounting up himself. 'But let's hurry. There's no time to lose. When Queen Guinevere rode south for Camelot, I thought I was a happy man. But would to God she were still in Castle Joyful today and not where she is!' He looked at Lancelot, knowing he shared the same fear. 'If Mordred has stolen the crown, just what does he mean to do with the Queen?'

Fifteen

SNAKE IN
THE GRASS

*M*ordred wanted everything that was Arthur's.
Not just his kingdom and his power, but his
friends, his castle and his wife. So he spread the word
that Arthur was dead, and that he, as Arthur's natural
born son, was heir to it all.

When he told Guinevere, she looked at him with a
face as blank as a castle wall. But she did not say, 'Liar. I
just came from his camp. Arthur is not dead.'

When he told her she must marry him or lose the title
of Queen, she looked at him with a face as pale as
marble, but she did not say, 'I should sooner lose my life
than marry you.' She did not spit in his face or make
comparison between Mordred and Arthur. She simply
inclined her head and said, 'If I am to be married, I must
buy a wedding veil. I shall ride to London now.'

Mordred hugged himself in his two arms and paced the length of Camelot fingering the hangings, the carved furniture. 'Mine,' he said. 'All mine.'

'With whose help?'

He turned quickly and saw Morgan le Fay sitting on the Queen's throne. In one hand was a silver mirror, in the other a comb.

'Morgan. I didn't hear you come in.'

'Nor did Arthur the night I stole Excalibur's scabbard.'

'Ah yes.'

'Nor did Merlin when I conjured him to love Nimue.'

'That was clever,' said Mordred.

'It was I who brought Balin his second fateful sword, and I who brought Lancelot here, knowing he would steal the love of Guinevere. I, the Lady of the Woods.'

'You were always subtle,' said Mordred.

'But you mean to marry Guinevere rather than me,' said Morgan.

Mordred recoiled, as if stung by a snake. He had hoped to keep his marriage plans secret for a while. 'The King of Albion has to marry the fairest woman in the land. It has been so for a thousand years.'

'You told me once that *I* was the fairest,' said Morgan. But she was not seething or shouting. Her long white fingers did not look charged with spiteful magic. She simply glanced, from time to time, into the silver mirror.

'I shall repay your help,' Mordred said. (There was no point in promising more. Morgan could read the future. What did she see there? A King Mordred, with Guinevere enthroned beside him? Or did she really fool herself that Mordred would put an ageing witch on the throne of Albion?) 'You shall have your revenge, my darling dear, when I fight Arthur and kill him.'

But to his astonishment, she said. 'Don't fight him, Mordred.'

'Not fight Arthur? You think he'll let me take his kingdom from him without a fight?'

'I think, if he has a brain in his head, he won't start a war that will wash away Albion in a sea of blood. But there . . . Who can judge what *men* will do?' She got up and sauntered slowly out of the room. Her fingers stroked the rim of the Round Table, its seams all sagging, its brass binding hanging loose, its surface too uneven now for a cup to be set down on it without spilling. 'By the way, Mordred . . .'

'Yes, my dear, my dove?'

'If you suppose Guinevere has gone to London to buy a wedding veil, you're a bigger fool than I took you for.'

When she had gone, he noticed her mirror face-down

on the Table, and picked it up, to groom his black moustache. But looking in the glass, he threw it away from him on to the stone floor. It was not *his* reflection but *hers*, still lingering there, dim and sallow, filling the frame. And round her brow, like a crown of willow, a green snake coiled its diamond scales.

Mordred thought about what Morgan had said, then called for his fastest horse. He rode full-tilt for London, following in the hoofprints of Guinevere's white mare. But though he galloped his horse to exhaustion, he came to the Tower of London just as its great gates closed against him.

'Come out, Guinevere, and be married to the King of Albion!' he bawled, banging on the door.

Guinevere appeared at a window high above him. 'I am already married to the King of Albion. And here I stay, Mordred, safe from villains like you, until he has crushed you underfoot like the worm you are!'

When the people of Albion found out that Arthur was not dead, many rallied to his flag. But to his followers Mordred promised counties and boroughs, estates and charters, gold and silver and posts of power if they would fight on his side. The greedy and the landless, the young and the wicked agreed, saying, 'In the end the old are always destroyed by the young. Arthur's time is past and Mordred's hour has come.'

At last two armies of equal size came face to face. The River Camlan moved between them like a slow, silver serpent. The evening sun slid down the sky like a clot of blood. Only one more night kept them apart.

Arthur had a dream that night, a nightmare of such awful clarity that he cried out loud in his sleep. He dreamed he was tied to a wheel as large as a hill. He dreamed himself to be on the topmost rim – so high that he could see across seven counties, and knew that every tree, every castle, every distant city was his and would come if he called. Presently, though, the wheel began to turn. Down and down he was carried, struggling with the ropes that bound him, until the soft mud of a cart-rut swallowed him, and the weight of the wheel was crushing his feet, his legs, his back, his face . . .

He woke up with his bedding rent to shreds around him, and his pageboys staring at him with big, frightened eyes. They asked if he was ill.

'The Wheel of Fortune has gone round,' was all he said. When Gawain put his head round the tent flap, Arthur beckoned him in. 'If we fight today, we shall die, Gawain! Not just me, not just a hundred men. Thousands will die, and Albion will be a land of widows and orphaned children. Summon Mordred to parley, and let us settle this thing the woman's way, by talking.'

His words pleased the men outside. They sighed a sigh of pure relief and joy. Ten thousand men lived in hope of seeing their wives and children again, and of leaving that place alive. Some even began to dance and sing for joy.

Under blowing banners, the leaders of the two armies rode towards the ford. Father and son met with the river at their feet, both bound by their word-of-honour that no weapon would be drawn while the peace talks lasted.

'I feel no love for you, Mordred,' Arthur began, 'though God knows a father should.'

'I feel no love for you, Dragonheaded Arthur,' said Mordred, 'and the Devil knows I never will.'

'If this battle is fought, Mordred, ten thousand knights will die today. How can Albion be the better for that?'

Mordred stroked his moustache with finger and thumb and smiled. 'And if this battle is *not* fought today, how shall *I* be the better for that?'

'I shall share my kingdom with you,' said the King wearily.

Outwardly, Mordred showed no excitement, but his horse skipped and splashed in the shallow water, trembling and sweating and chewing its bit. Arthur could see his son's black eyes fill up with all the things he would ask for, all the demands he would make.

Just then, out from under a stone a viper slid to sip from the lip of the Camlan. It found in its way an iron shod foot, and bit the ankle above it. Without a thought, the bitten knight drew his sword to kill the snake. The sun's rays caught on the silver blade . . .

Then it was: 'Treachery!'

'Ambush!'

'A trick!'

'To arms!'

Both armies surged forward. The horses in the ford took fright and shied, clouding the scene in spray. Amid shouted curses and recriminations, the parley banners slumped into the river and were shredded by the hooves of charging horses.

Sixteen

IN THE END

In the great hall of Camelot, the Round Table fell from its plinth like a cartwheel from its axle. It crashed to the floor and rolled on its rim, round and round and round, springing every seam, splitting and splintering, overturning the Seat of Mortal Danger.

On the battlefield of Camlan, the fighting men of Albion cut one another to pieces. The young did not have the experience and skill of the older knights, the older knights did not have the energy or stamina to outlive the long day. The river ran red, the grass was flayed away and the earth beneath was trampled into mud. The silver lying in the muddy ruts was not water, but the armour of fallen knights.

Like a forest ravaged by fire, they all fell: Kay, Pellinore, Tor, Lamorak, Aglovale, Lucan, Bors, Lionel, Urry . . .

Lancelot.

By dusk a handful were left standing, like blasted trees blackened and motionless, leaning at crazy angles to the skyline. One was Arthur, one Mordred, one Sir Bedevere.

'All day I have hunted you, Mordred!' croaked Arthur, 'but you've slipped out of my grasp like a stoat. Stand and fight!'

Mordred was unwilling. He looked around him at the kingdom he had wanted; there was no one left to rule, no army to command, no hands to crown him. Morgan le Fay's magic had worked no wonders on his behalf. She had abandoned him to his fate. Only Death had triumphed on the banks of the Camlan. Mordred was left with nothing but a superstitious dread of raising his sword against his rightful king. Arthur came wading through the dead towards him. He turned to run.

'Uncle!' A hand grabbed at Arthur's ankle. It was Gawain. The King knelt down beside him. 'I am dying, my lord,' said Gawain. 'I was struck on the same wound Lancelot gave me outside Castle Joyful, and this time it won't heal. All this is my doing, uncle! My revenge opened the way for Mordred.'

'Peace, nephew. It was our destiny.'

'But I must make peace with Lancelot! I was wrong to break with him! I was wrong!'

'Peace, peace, Gawain,' said the King. 'Today ten thousand knights are making their peace in Heaven. And you and Lancelot and your brothers and sons can sit down at Christ's Round Table and break bread with the angels. Good quest, my brave knight.' As Gawain slipped out of his arms, the green sash around his armour snapped and came away in Arthur's hand.

Excalibur seemed an unbearable weight to drag across the battlefield, but the sight of Mordred stumbling away fired Arthur with the energy he needed. 'Stand, coward! Stand and fight!' he gasped, and Mordred finally turned.

They fought like men threshing grain, their blades crashing down, metal on metal. But Excalibur was shaped for Mordred's heart, as surely as a key is for a lock. It was Arthur who struck the mortal blow.

Sometimes a boar, speared in the hunt, runs on up the spear and gores the hunter who has killed it. Despite his death wound, Mordred came on. He drove his sword between Arthur's cuirass and helmet, and crashed up against him, chest to chest. His black moustache brushed Arthur's cheek. 'No victors!' he hissed in the King's ear.

When Sir Bedevere came across the King, Mordred lay dead across his legs, but Arthur was hardly less pale. 'I'll run for help – a convent, a town – I'll find somewhere you can rest – women to nurse you . . .'

Arthur held up a hand. 'I am dying, Bedevere. Carry me into those woods. There's something that must be done before I die.'

Without knowing how, Sir Bedevere got the King on to his back, and they entered a wood. Its paths were no more than a tangle of deer tracks, and the daylight was fading fast. But Arthur directed Bedevere as though he knew every tree and bush. The boughs groaned and the underbush stirred; the leaves shivered as though rain were coming. It was very cold.

'God knows, I want to obey you, master,' Bedevere panted, 'but I can't go on. My wounds . . . my strength is all used up.'

'Just a little farther, friend,' urged Arthur. But the knight dropped to his knees under the intolerable weight.

Arthur leaned his back against a tree and shut his eyes. 'You must go for me, then. Take Excalibur to the lake. Throw her in.'

On all fours amid the leaf mould, Bedevere fought for breath. 'Lake? What lake?'

'The lake beyond those trees.' Arthur pushed Excalibur across the ground to Bedevere, who got painfully to his feet.

And yes. He could see it now! Shining in the newly risen moon. A lake so large that its far shore was out of sight. It might almost have been an inlet of the sea. Mistletoe hung over the water, white like bridal wreaths.

Bedevere scuffed his way to the shore, dragging the heavy sword. The moon gleamed on the jewels inlaid in its hilt, the exquisite tracery chased on its blade. Throw it in the lake? What if the King recovered and needed it

again? Where would Camelot be without Excalibur?

So Bedevere hid the sword under the dead leaves, and went back to Arthur.

'Did you throw it?' whispered Arthur.

'I—'

'What did you see?'

'See? I saw the grebes run and the fish scatter.'

'Then you're a deceitful rogue. Go back and throw the sword into the lake, as I commanded you.'

Bedevere broke into a stumbling run and returned to the lake's beach. But as he drew Excalibur from its hiding place, the moon flashed on its bright blade and the rubies in the hilt burned like fiery coals. When he went to throw it, the weight in his hand was perfection. How could he destroy such a sword? The King might already be dead. Excalibur and Bedevere himself were all that remained of the Golden Age. He stuck the weapon into a bush and walked back.

'Did you throw the sword?' whispered Arthur, without opening his eyes.

'Yes.'

'And what did you see?'

'See? I saw the water drops fly and the weed stir,' said Bedevere.

'Liar. Traitor. Must I do it myself, then?' Arthur tried to get up.

'No! No! No! I'll do it! I'll do it now!' Bedevere ran all

the way, pulled Excalibur from the bush and swung it once, twice, three times round his head before letting it fly out over the water. When tears filled his eyes, he cursed them: 'I shall see nothing!'

But the tears cleared to show him the surface of the lake and the moon's white face reflected in it. Through the moon's reflection broke a hand, a woman's hand. It caught the hilt of Excalibur, brandished it three times in the moonlight, then drew it down into the deep dark.

'What did you see?' asked Arthur.

'I saw the Lady of the Lake take back the sword she lent you,' said Bedevere gently, unbuckling Arthur's remaining armour and scattering it about in bright shards. The King gave a great sigh of satisfaction. When Sir Bedevere made to brush the hair out of his eyes, Arthur's face was as cold as any stone.

Through the trees came a splash of oars. Bedevere stood up and glimpsed three women shipping the black oars of a long rowing boat, running it ashore. He recognized one as Morgan le Fay.

'Have you not done with him yet, you carrion witch?' he blared at her. 'Do you want to pick the flesh off his bones?'

She looked at him with her green eyes, and he saw there, to his amazement, no evil menace, no seething envy. 'Time has run its course, Sir Bedevere,' she said calmly. 'The world's loss today overshadows petty hates and futile loves, as a mountain overshadows a tree. Albion is empty today of Good and Bad alike. The giants and dragons are dead; the heroes are gone, too. Bear witness to the world that was, and to the history of its heroes. That is your only duty now.'

The three women picked up Arthur as if he weighed no more than a sword.

'Where are you taking him?'

'To the Isle of Avalon, to rest and recover from his wounds.'

'But he's—'

'Sleeping, yes,' said Morgan the Faery. 'So speak low, Sir Bedevere and tread softly. It is not time yet for the King to wake again.'

They placed Arthur in the boat, on cushions and amid candles whose smoke smelled as sweet as a field of burning flowers. The oars cut silver gules in the oily lake, and like a black swan the boat glided out from the shore.

Bedevere watched it till it sailed out of sight. The leaves around him trembled at the approach of rain.

OSCAR WILDE STORIES FOR CHILDREN

Illustrated by P. J. Lynch

Beautifully illustrated by award-winning artist, Oscar Wilde's timeless tales are brought to life for a whole new generation of children. This classic story collection includes *The Happy Prince*, *The Selfish Giant* and many more.

Another title from Hodder Children's Books

ROBIN OF SHERWOOD

Written by Michael Morpurgo

In this magical spine-tingling story, the heroic tale of Robin Hood is retold as never before. After a fierce storm, a boy of today discovers a human skull beneath the roots of an upturned oak tree – and is suddenly thrown into the ancient world of Sherwood Forest. Plunged into a world of poverty and oppression, Robin joins the Outcasts, a motley bunch of misfits, beggars and albinos – feared and hated for their difference and fighting for survival in the depths of Sherwood Forest.

Michael Morpurgo's skill is to unfold a compelling drama of horror, humour, bravery and betrayal where dream is mixed with reality in this most atmospheric and original retelling of a popular tale.

Another title from Hodder Children's Books

JOHN BUNYAN'S A PILGRIM'S PROGRESS

*Retold by Geraldine McCaughrean and
illustrated by Jason Cockcroft*

On his journey of a lifetime to the City of Gold,
Christian meets an extraordinary cast of characters,
such as the terrible Giant Despair and the monster
Apollyon. Together with Hopeful, his steadfast
companion, he survives snipers and mantraps, the
Great Bog, Vanity Fair, Lucre Hill and Doubting
Castle. But will he find the courage to cross the final
river to the City of Gold and his salvation.

Winner of the Blue Peter Book Awards: A special
book to keep forever and the overall winner of the
Blue Peter Book of the Year.

CELTIC MYTHS

Retold by Sam McBratney

Best-selling author Sam McBratney recreates the magic of Celtic legends in this fascinating book of retellings. This collection contains tales from English, Irish, Scottish and Welsh folklore. Their other worldliness ranges from the fantastically gruesome to the hauntingly beautiful and they are full of mystery and enchantment.

SHAKESPEARE'S STORIES

*Written by Beverley Birch and
illustrated by James Mayhew*

Shakespeare's Stories includes five of Shakespeare's best-loved plays beautifully and evocatively retold by Beverley Birch: *Romeo & Juliet, Macbeth, Twelfth Night, A Midsummer Night's Dream* and *Julius Caesar*.

James Mayhew's stunning illustrations perfectly capture the characters, the drama and the atmosphere in all the stories in this delightful gift book.

SHAKESPEARE'S TALES

*Written by Beverley Birch and
illustrated by Stephen Lambert*

Shakespeare's Tales includes another four of Shakespeare's best-loved plays, retold again by Beverley Birch in her distinctive and compelling style: *Hamlet, Antony & Cleopatra, Othello* and *The Tempest.*

Stephen Lambert's haunting illustrations perfectly capture the drama and the tragedy in all the stories in this superb gift book.